DEMONIC
and other tales

the short fiction of
Garon Cockrell

doorQ Publishing I Playa del Rey, California

Published in the USA by
doorQ Publishing
8675 Falmouth Ave #306
Playa del Rey, CA 90293
www.doorq.com

ISBN-10: 0692324860
ISBN-13: 978-0692324868

Cover photo by Saiuri

Printed in the United States of America

Dedication

To my parents for never saying don't do what you love.

To Jason who kept me on my path and never stopped having faith in me.

This is but the first step and with you at my side there will be many more to take. 143.

Table of Contents

Demonic

CASEY CARROLL STOOD ALONE OUTSIDE THE RECORD STORE. HE had his hands firmly in his pockets gripping a lone water bottle cap. His black hair was stringy and greasy, and he had thick glasses with ancient blue frames - a gift from his long dead grandfather. It was getting late in the afternoon now and the crowd had thinned considerably. Casey still remained by the window of the record store staring inside at the reason he left his room that day.

Her name was Bella, and to Casey, she was the most beautiful creature on earth. Her third straight #1 single was playing on every radio station and she was embarking on a tour of record stores and radio stations. For some reason, Bella's management had booked her in a small record store in the city of Bricks Hollow, Maine. This nearly being Casey's doorstep, he felt this was, quite frankly, Fate.

Unfortunately, Casey had been unable to work up the nerve to actually go inside and speak with Bella. So instead, he stood outside, his hands in his pockets, playing with the bottle cap she had dropped on her way into the store. As the line grew smaller, Casey found himself becoming more and more nervous. He watched as Bella signed posters, CDs, and any number of trinkets. His heart thudded in his chest as he watched her scrawl her elegant signature.

Finally, the last group of people entered the store and Casey found his nerve. He turned and walked towards the door. He hadn't taken three steps before crashing into a very large, very black, bodyguard.

"'Scuse me," Casey mumbled and tried to step around the body guard.

"Uh-uh." The body guard looked down at Casey and put his hand against his chest. He gave a heave that sent Casey sprawling to the ground, "Meet and greet's over, bub."

"But, I've been waiting…" Casey started.

"Uh-uh. You've been standin' front of the window for the past 3 hours. Meet and greet's over. Go home."

"But I didn't get to meet Bella." Casey's voice was hard, a hint of anger underneath the layer of fear he was feeling.

"And you aren't going to. So stand up, turn around and go home. Maybe you can touch yourself to make up for the shame of being a pussy. Now get the fuck outta here." Casey blinked. "I said get the fuck outta here, crazy." Casey blinked again. The bodyguard chuckled and turned away.

Casey launched himself like a rocket. His face contorted in a mask of rage, foam spewing from his mouth.

"YOU CAN'T TALK TO ME THAT WAY YOU MONKEY MOTHER FUCKER!" Casey screamed and leapt onto the bodyguard's shoulders. He tried to get his arms around his neck but the bodyguard simply grabbed Casey's wrists and tossed him aside.

"Monkey? That's racist. You're a racist punk." The bodyguard delivered one punch directly to the tip of Casey's nose, shattering it and sending a spray of blood, and Casey's glasses, through the air. Again, Casey found himself sprawled on the sidewalk.

"Go home, you white bread honky psycho mama's boy. I don't ever want to lay eyes on you again. You damned piece of garbage." The bodyguard kicked Casey and walked back into the store.

Casey stood up slowly, holding his ribs and wincing in pain. He picked his glasses up from the sidewalk and put them on. He wiped his arm across his nose and was rewarded with a white hot burst of pain. Through his watering eyes he saw Bella looking out at him. In her eyes, he saw concern and longing and he desperately wanted to go to her as much as it seemed she wanted to run to his aid. In reality, Bella's eyes were wide with fear, but that would never have entered his mind. He believed Bella would fall for him the moment they met. Looking at her now, shimmering through his watering eyes, he knew that more than ever. With warmth blossoming in his chest and a smile on his face, Casey left for home. He wasn't worried about catching her before she left town.

He knew what hotel she was staying at.

***

"Tell me that was a misunderstanding and you didn't just beat the shit out of one of my fans." Bella had her hands planted firmly on her hips. The last of her fans had left the store twenty minutes ago and Bella couldn't get the sight of the bloodied boy in the window out of her mind.

"Well, I wouldn't say I beat the shit out of him."

"Great. That's all I need to see in the tabloids. My bodyguard beating teenage fans half to death."

"He was lookin' at you like you were donuts at a fat camp."

"Everyone looks at me like that."

"This was different."

"Teddy, you are too protective of me. Next time, just… try to avoid bloodying the crazy fans, ok?"

"Fo' sho' boss."

Bella pulled on her coat and flipped her hair over the collar. "Can we go now?"

***

"That motherfucker called me crazy, I'll show him crazy." Casey walked around the side of his house into the overgrown back yard.

The back door burst open and his father screamed out at him, "Mow this lawn!"

Casey looked up at the old man. He was 60 years old, his hair fully grey and falling out in patches. He was carrying a thick leather belt in his hand.

"Mow it yourself, you old fart!" Casey turned and pushed through the thick weeds to the decrepit shed ahead of him.

"What did you say to me, boy?" His father stepped off the porch.

"I said…" Casey yanked open the shed doors, "mow it yourself, you FUCKING OLD PIECE OF HORSESHIT FART!"

"You bastard, you evil little bastard," His father came up on him quickly, the belt swinging in an arch towards Casey's back. It struck with a vicious slap. Casey did not flinch. He slowly turned around just as his father swung the belt again. Casey caught the strap in his hand and yanked it from his father's grip.

"No more." Casey said. He let the belt dangle from his hand, the thick heavy buckle swinging dangerously. He swung the belt and watched as the buckle sliced into his father's cheek. A thick chunk of flesh was gouged away by the tooth of the buckle. His father howled in pain and stumbled back. Casey reared back and struck again. This time the tooth of the belt impaled his father's eye and pulled it out with a pop. Casey did not stop. He swung and swung and did not stop until his father was a bleeding pulp on the ground. "No more," Casey repeated and dropped the belt.

He walked into the shed, oblivious to the blood on his arms and face, nor feeling the pain in his nose any longer. His emotions were overruled by his love for Bella. He could think of nothing more. Not even when he heard his mother screaming. Not even as he pulled the dull axe from its perch between a hatchet and sickle on the shed wall. Not even when he went to shut her up.

He felt only his love for Bella and he knew, in just a short time, he would have her.

***

It was dark now. The town shut down, its citizens asleep long before this midnight hour. Casey, however, was walking down the center of Main Street towards the Horseman Inn, the ritziest hotel in town. It was as ritzy as you could get for $35 a night, anyway. It was a four story historical building recently purchased by some lackluster hotel chain. They just hadn't changed the sign yet.

Casey stood outside the hotel. He had both the hatchet and the sickle hung on his belt. He carried the axe in his hand, still dripping with gore from teaching his mother her manners.

"It's time for love, mmmm baby, let's get together for love." He walked towards the door singing his favorite Bella song. He pushed the doors open and stepped into the hotel lobby.

"Jesus H!" the desk clerk screamed, trying to reach for the phone when he saw Casey, bloodied and crazed, step inside the lobby. Casey halted him in his tracks when he threw the axe across the room, burying the blade into the clerk's skull.

"Love baby, you and I, together forever in loooooove." Casey walked around the front desk and typed Bella's name into the computer. No results. He thought a moment and then simply looked through the most recent check-ins. There were two. A man named Hubert Finkle and a woman named Lindsay Duff. Not entirely clever on her part, but Casey could forgive that. The log showed their rooms as 304 and 307. He resumed his singing and walked over to the elevator, pausing only to yank the axe from the desk clerk's cranium. It took two pulls to free it.

He stepped into the elevator and heard the Muzak version of Bella's latest single playing over the elevator speakers. He smiled. The elevator doors slid closed with a ding and he began to ascend.

***

Of Bella's three bodyguards, two of them, Barry and Sean, were currently snoring in room 307. Teddy, the third and head bodyguard, was roughly fucking Bella in room 304. The noises coming from her mouth sounded nothing like the corny pop songs that had taken her to the top of the charts.

"You like this bitch?" Teddy grunted as he impaled himself into her.

"Oh Jesus fuck yes!"

The scene looked a bit like a bear on top of a chipmunk, but Bella was clearly enjoying herself. Her legs and ankles were tightly wrapped around Teddy's neck. Neither of them took any notice to the door opening or Casey walking into the room. They did, however, notice the howl of agony that erupted from him when he saw what they were doing.

Teddy pulled himself off Bella, his cock rapidly deflating. He had no time to react before Casey was hacking away at him.

"GET AWAY FROM HER!! GETAWAYGETAWAY-GETAWAY!"

Bella shrieked in horror as she watched Casey dismember Teddy, chopping until the axe handle broke, leaving the blade imbedded in the side of Teddy's head. He turned to Bella and looked longingly at her.

"I'm sorry you had to see that, Bella. He was hurting you and I had to protect you."

Bella's eyes widened to an impossible size.

"It's ok. I'm here now." Casey began to sing again, "It's time for love, mmmm baby, let's get together for love."

Bella began shrieking all over again.

Barry didn't hear Bella screaming as Casey hacked Teddy to pieces; neither, for that matter, did Sean. The only reason he heard her the second time was because he had woken up with the worst case of the shits he had ever experienced. In fact, he was sitting on the toilet when the shrieking began. He cleaned up as best as he could and yanked his pants on. He managed to remember to grab his gun and kick Sean's bed to wake him before he ran out the door and into the hall. His room was just a few doors down from Bella's so he could see the small river of blood running from under her door.

"Oh shit," he said as he approached. He pushed the door open and saw Casey straddling Bella. He was digging the sickle into her gut and crying as he sang her song. Barry made it no farther. He simply passed out and cracked his head on the edge of the entertainment center.

Casey paid him no mind. He straightened up and realized what he was doing. His hands were covered in Bella's blood. A string of her intestine was wrapped around his wrist. He gently unraveled it and stuck it back inside the gaping hole in her stomach and then, leaning forward, kissed her softly on her rapidly cooling lips.

"I didn't mean for this to happen," he whispered. "Please forgive me." he ran his fingers along her blood soaked hair. "You just make me crazy, sweetheart."

"What the fuck!" Sean stepped into the room. He was pointing his 9mm at Casey. "What have you done? You... look at this! This blood! Everywhere! You killed her! Her guts are out!" Sean's hand started shaking. He put his free hand against his mouth in an attempt to hold in the vomit. His skin seemed to turn translucent as he took in the scene before him. Casey simply climbed off the bed and walked to him. Sean was too weak to pull the trigger; his eyes had glazed over. Casey snatched the gun from him and put a bullet in Sean's eye. That was that. He stepped over Sean's body and into the hall towards the elevator, and pressed the down button. He continued to hum Bella's song as he waited.

Behind him, a figure stepped out of the hotel room. It was Bella, but truth be told, she was no longer Bella. Her face had contorted into a beastly grimace and her legs now resembled the limbs of a goat. She was naked, but her breasts were now covered with a dense black fur. Two thick black horns emerged from her forehead. She had long jagged teeth in a too large mouth. Behind her, a tail twitched in the air.

Casey hummed the song and casually glanced over his shoulder at the beast emerging from the hotel room. He looked back at the elevator doors and then the humming ceased. He spun around and faced the demon with a look of horror on his face.

"What's the matter?" The demon asked in a deep growling

voice. It was caressing its breasts. Its hands, more like claws, ran down between its goat like legs. "Don't you love me anymore?"

Casey felt his bladder release.

"Don't you want me?"

Casey clawed at the elevator door. His hair began turning stark white.

"Love me!" The demon howled and reached forward to brush Casey's cheek.

Casey screamed.

The elevator chimed and the doors slid open. Casey collapsed into the carriage at the feet of a tall man in a dark silk business suit.

"You are a troublesome one, Casey." The man said with a slight British accent.

"Help me! There's a monster!"

"Do shut up." The man bent over, picked Casey up by the scruff and set him on his feet.

"You've caused me some trouble here tonight, Casey, namely by decimating my primary investment. I'll have to find something to replace her. She has made me quite a bit of money. Now, how am I going to fix this?"

"I – I don't understand."

The demon stepped into the elevator, only now, she was Bella again, nude and gutted as before. She turned her wrath on Casey.

"You killed me, you dumb bastard. I can't very well be a pop star with my fucking guts hanging out! It will take years to get rid of the scarring!"

"Hush, Bella. Let me think." The man in the suit appeared to be contemplating the situation.

Casey was at his breaking point. This was too much. "WHAT THE FUCK IS GOING ON HERE?" he shouted.

The businessman sighed.

"She may be incredibly sexy, but she is hardly the greatest singer in the world. How do you suppose she became so famous, such a chart-topping artist? Admittedly, in hindsight, it was foolish of me to send her to this ass fuck town but, what I lack in foresight I do make up for in business sense. I should have seen something like this coming, but I've been so busy…"

Sensing Casey's confusion, Bella spoke up.

"I sold my soul to him to become famous, stupid. He is the devil. Satan. Y'know, Lacifer?"

The man in the suit looked annoyed. "It's Lucifer, you silly cow."

Bella shrugged.

The Devil looked again at Casey. "Now then," he crouched and put a hand on Casey's shoulder, "Shall we make ourselves a little deal?"

***

Somewhere in Middle America…

"Oh my God!!!" The girl squealed. She ran through the hallway of Ford Middle School toward a group of similarly dressed girls. They were all huddled around each other. The girl in the center held a CD in her hand.

"Look, he autographed it! Isn't he the cutest?!"

The CD showed the four young attractive guys who made up the boy band "Kick Start" on the cover. Each was posed looking dreamily at the camera. The one in the center had dark hair and a slightly sad expression.

"I can't believe you met him! He is the hottest guy ever. I can't believe it! KC touched you! He touched you and signed your CD!"

The girls continued their chatter and giggling until they noticed a short red haired girl opening a locker a few feet away.

"Is that her?" one whispered.

"Yes. She's a junior. What a skank."

"I can't believe she's here. She used to be famous! I thought she was older."

Bella heard them talking, yet didn't care. She was content to wait. She would just go through the motions until her master called on her. He would call on her. She knew it. He couldn't use that psycho Casey forever. Besides, boy bands never lasted. They would fade out just like all the others and He would need another tool. Then it would be her time for a glorious comeback. It was just a matter of time before it was her turn to shine again.

"Oh my god KC is SOOOO CUTE!!!" All of the girls giggled, having forgotten all about Bella. She wanted to kill them and bathe in their blood. Instead, she scowled and slammed her locker shut.

It was just a matter of time.

Eggs

FELICIA HARDEN STOOD IN THE BACK OF THE GROCERY STORE staring at a shelf full of eggs. She was sixty-five years old, moderately healthy, and generally a happy and sane individual. And so, it was rather strange that the eggs were speaking to her, screaming at her for that matter. They were begging for her to rescue them.

A young woman approached and after glancing at Felicia she grabbed a box of farm fresh eggs which elicited a chorus of terror from the occupants.

"Do you hear them?" Felicia asked the woman.

She looked at Felicia with confusion spread over her face, "Excuse me?"

Felicia realized that the woman could not hear the terrible din coming from that cardboard box. She lowered her head and pushed her cart away from the screaming eggs and the bewildered young woman.

***

At home, Felicia sat alone in her living room. She had her hands folded in her lap and was staring at the wall across from her. The wall was full of pictures of her family. She looked at the photos of her children; Tanya, grown with children of her own, and Nick, sweet Nick, who was killed when he was seventeen. The photos also featured her husband, Richard.

He was never quite right after Nick's death. He took to the bottle and began hitting Felicia and Tanya. Not hard, he never left a mark; he just took to slapping when he got upset. Once day he closed his hand and punched Felicia. He wasn't a strong man and Felicia was more frightened than anything. But Richard was so ashamed of himself that he fled the house. The grief and shame was too much for him to bear and so he threw himself from the Cross Street Bridge and was crushed beneath the 3:05 to Tulsa.

Now, Felicia was alone.

Alone, except for the eggs.

They were calling her from the fridge. They knew her name and were shouting it incessantly. The voices were filled with such terror that it was maddening.

Felicia looked towards the kitchen and wiped a tear from her cheek.

"Save our friends."

Felicia cocked her head slightly. The voice was so familiar to her.

"Please save them."

Felicia stood up quickly and rushed into the kitchen, "Nick?"

She pulled open the fridge, "Nick?" She reached into the fridge and picked up the carton of eggs. The screaming was almost unbearable but that one voice, Nick's voice, was still clear. Felicia opened the lid.

The eggs were still but the screaming continued.

"Please save them." Nick said again, his voice cutting through the screams of his peers. The center egg twitched and a small crack opened. A thin red line oozed from the fissure.

"The pain!" Nick hissed.

The crack deepened and a chunk of shell fell away exposing a small, red, beating heart.

"Save them from the pain!" Nick shrieked,

Felicia dropped the carton. The eggs shattered and spilled thick red blood across the floor. Felicia looked down at twelve beating hearts on the floor before her.

That moment was the last for Felicia Harden. The site of those tiny hearts beating destroyed her mind. Almost as if her sanity was released along with her bladder. The results of which were mixing with the blood on the kitchen linoleum.

There were only two thoughts running through her head at that moment. The first was of saving the rest of the eggs from the store.

The second was of her dead husband's gun.

***

She shuffled into the grocery store in a daze. Her dress was stained with urine, the smell of which rapidly reached nearby patrons.

Felicia grabbed a cart and pushed it towards the coolers at the back of the store. She bumped into a display of baby food, sending the jars exploding onto the floor. She did not feel the glass shards cut into her legs. She could only hear the eggs now, calling for her, begging for salvation.

"Mrs. Hardy?"

Jackson Simmons did not wake up this morning expecting to deal with a woman who seemed to have lost her mind. All he cared about was trim and weed, and this stock job gave him enough money for both. So in truth, he really didn't care why this batty loon was walking through the grocery store with bleeding legs and a piss stained dress. Normally, he would have just ignored her but for some reason he felt like he should speak to her. Fate apparently wanted his life to be short.

One can never be satisfied with their last words, and this was especially true in Jackson's case because, unless you count the slight moan and sputtering, Felicia Harden's name was the last he would ever speak.

At the sound of her name, Felicia whipped out her dead husband's gun and blew off half of Jackson's face. She paid no attention to the ghost smile of his exposed skull nor to the gore slipping down the shelf of Huggies behind him.

Felicia pushed the cart forward, gingerly stepping past Jackson's twitching legs and slipped slightly in the widening pool of blood. She was dimly aware of screaming and the pounding of footsteps but these were secondary to the eggs. They were calling for her. She reached the end of the aisle and turned to the left.

There they were; the eggs. She rushed forward and slammed the cart into the cooler at a full run. She felt something snap in her chest. It felt like something had broken and was now ripping into her lungs. Each breath sent a searing pain throughout her torso.

She ignored the pain and starting placing egg cartons into her shopping cart. The eggs were cheering now, ecstatic to be so close to freedom.

"Don't worry, I'll get you out of here. You'll be safe now."

All she heard was the elation coming from the cartons as she stacked them in her cart. She of course did not notice the near silence pervading the rest of the store. The only sound being the soft adult contemporary music spilling from the speakers in the ceiling. The store had emptied of people, all of whom were now gathered outside. They all had rushed out when Felicia had blown the face off of Jackson Simmons. Now she was alone with the eggs. The happiness in the voices was causing tears to run down her face. She had never heard such relief, such joy.

"Mrs. Harden." There was a new voice, and it was stern and deep. Felicia straightened and slowly turned to face Reginald Topher. He was a slightly grey haired, overweight black man. He stood peaking around a display of Rice Krispies. He was afraid, that was obvious, but doing his best to keep it from his voice. He was the store manager.

"Mr. Topher. I'd ask you to leave me to collect my friends here. I will meet you directly at the checkout counter just as soon as I've finished here."

"But Mrs. Harden, you've shot a man."

Felicia placed another egg carton into her cart. There were only a dozen or so remaining. Her eyes at that moment were completely clear almost as if her sanity had returned briefly, but then it was gone and her eyes went wild again. She raised the gun and squeezed off another round. A box of Rice Krispies exploded sending the rice puffs showering to the ground.

Satisfied that Reginald would not bother her again, she set about rescuing the last of the eggs. Her cart was full and surprisingly easy to push after she placed the last carton inside. The eggs were sighing contently. Some were crying with joy, others whooping and laughing. Felicia felt like a hero and was far too happy to notice the blood streaming out of her eyes like thick red tears.

"Thank you, Mother." Nick said to her.

Felicia began to cry as her cart veered towards a wall of soda. It bounced off the shelves and she centered herself and her cart. Her vision was blurring now. A watery red film covered her sight. She saw several blurred shapes rushing towards her. They meant to stop her from rescuing the eggs. She knew this.

"STOP THEM!" Nick screamed. The eggs responded with equal terror.

The police officers that rushed into the store had drawn their guns but when the weird voices came from Felicia's mouth they hesitated. This old woman was piss stained and bleeding from her eyes and now was speaking to herself in different voices. She was clearly insane and none of them wanted to have her blood on their hands.

It was this hesitation that caused young Billy Burke's life to end. It was his second day on the force and his last. Felicia had unleashed her gun again and plugged him straight between the eyes. The back of his head exploded in the face of his partner, twenty five year veteran Jeffrey Morgan. He would spend the next ten years trying to clean the young man's brains from his face before he decided to join him by leaping from the roof of the downtown library.

When she fired, Felicia snapped the cops from their temporary confusion. The seven remaining officers all emptied their guns. Out of 105 bullets fired, 90 would strike the hundreds of eggs in the basket. This was ten of the final forty five seconds of Felicia's life. In her head, she heard the din of the eggs as death took them all from her. She heard her son crying out again for her to save him but she could not.

The police heard all of this as well, only they heard it directly from the source: Felicia's mouth.

In the next second, the first bullet ripped into her chest and blew away the rib that was pressing into her lung. For a moment she could breathe normally until the next nine bullets chewed away at her.

The tenth, 105th, and final bullets were fired by one Miguel Sanchez. He was the first man of Mexican descent to become a peace officer in this small town. He did not fire when everyone else fired. He tensed, took aim, and steadied himself. He saw the wild bullets rip into the wall of egg cartons but his shot was true.

His bullet ripped into Felicia's forehead and blew the thick black infected tumor that now ran red with her blood clear out of the back of her head. It splattered heavily against a jar of chili and dropped to the cool linoleum with a smack.

Felicia smiled briefly at Miguel and he would swear for the next thirty seven years of his life that she whispered thank you before she fell dead over the cart full of ruined eggs.

Her blood dripped to the ground, mixing with the yellow yolks of the eggs.

Home Alone

JULIA KENNINGTON CHECKED HER MAKEUP IN THE MIRROR one last time. Tonight would be the first night she would go on a date in five years, and she was determined for things to go perfectly. That meant she had to look perfect. She turned to her son and smiled.

"Well?"

"Well what?" Kevin asked. He was twelve years old and was more interested in the game on his Nintendo DS than he was in the appearance of his mother.

"Don't be a brat. How do I look?"

He glanced at her briefly before returning to his game, "Fine."

Julia took that as a perfect compliment. She fished in her purse and pulled out a twenty dollar bill, "This is for pizza. I want the change back." She said, knowing full well it would disappear into Kevin's Playstation Fund jar, "Are you sure you'll be okay?"

"I'm twelve, Mom! You're only gonna be gone a few hours anyway."

"You call me if anything…"

"If anything, I know."

Julia ruffled Kevin's dark hair and kissed him on the forehead just as the doorbell rang, "Don't stay up too late!" She grabbed her purse and walked down the hall towards the front door. He heard her shoes clacking on the hard wood floor. Kevin watched as she opened the door and was kissed on the cheek by a man with graying hair. He waved at Kevin.

"Dick." Kevin whispered and pushed himself deeper into the couch.

"I love you, Kevin!" His mother called out and disappeared out the front door.

Kevin heard them laughing together as they walked down the front walk. He stood up and dropped his DS on the couch cushion. With a sigh, he walked out of the living room and to the front door. He peaked out the side window and watched as his mother climbed into Dick's car. He closed the door for her and jogged around to the driver's side. Kevin let the curtain fall and twisted the deadbolt locked. He looked up the stairs and into the dark hall to his left. He was home alone for the first time.

Thirty-eight minutes later Kevin was sitting again on the couch in the living room with a hot pizza in his lap and seven dollars in his pocket for the Playstation Fund. He flipped through the channels searching for something to watch while he ate his pizza.

He settled on some movie about a haunted house and hungrily

munched away while some ghost wreaked havoc on a young couple. As the film progressed, Kevin was growing more and more apprehensive by being alone in the house. The film was creeping him out to the point that he didn't even want to eat anymore. He shut his pizza box and set it aside. He glanced around for the TV remote and quickly flipped the horror movie off. The channel switched to a news broadcast and a dour looking woman was describing a prison break that had happened earlier in the evening.

"...has escaped. He was sentenced to life in prison five years ago after a being convicted of eight homicides. His crime spree was the stuff of horror films as he stalked and killed his victims while dressed up as a clown..."

Kevin quickly shut off the television, "REXIE!" He yelled and a Golden Retriever bounded into the room. The dog leapt over the back of the couch and landed firmly in Kevin's lap. Rexie licked Kevin's face leaving a trail of drool behind.

"Good boy!" Kevin wiped the spit away from his face and grabbed his DS, "Let's go to bed, Rexie!" He grabbed the cordless phone and walked out of the living room.

Kevin was pretending to be brave by turning off the lights in the lower floor of the house. In truth, he was getting more and more scared with each room that fell into darkness.

He paused briefly at the front door, which was directly in front of the stairs, and peaked out the side windows. The porch was empty and the street beyond was dark. Kevin checked the locks and finally satisfied he walked upstairs. Rexie followed obediently.

Kevin walked into his room and closed the door. He quickly changed into his pajamas and turned on the baseball bat lamp next to his bed. He turned off the ceiling light and climbed into bed. He played his DS for a bit longer while Rexie slept with his head across Kevin's leg until his eyes begin to droop and close against his will. Eventually, he could fight it no longer and closed his game and settled in for sleep.

He didn't know what caused him to awaken but his heart was pounding in his chest. He pushed back his blanket and pulled his legs from beneath Rexie's sleeping body. He slid out of bed and padded across the room to his window.

The street outside was quiet and dark. There were streetlights casting perfect round circles every few feet, but the rest of the street was shrouded in darkness. Kevin pressed his head closer to the glass and struggled to see further. His breath fogged the window. He wiped it away and squinted. That was when he saw it: two red semicircles, just barely inside a circle of light. They looked like the tips of a pair of plastic shoes, large floppy shoes.

"Clown shoes." Kevin whispered and jumped back from the window. He had to fight himself to keep from running back to his bed and hiding. Instead, he gathered his courage and looked out the window again. The small half circles of plastic clown shoe were gone. The street appeared empty, not a soul or a clown to be seen.

Kevin let out a sigh and returned to his bed. He must have imagined what he saw. He gently petted Rexie and moved to lay back down but stopped when he heard a knock at the front door. He leapt to his feet and looked at the clock. It clicked over to 12:35 just as another knock sounded at the door.

A deep growl came from Rexie and he barked loudly.

"Shh!" Kevin stepped to his door and quietly walked out into the hallway. He peeked around the corner so that he could see down the stairs, then stepped quietly as he slowly made his way down.

The knocking continued.

Rexie bolted past Kevin and was furiously barking at the front door. Kevin rushed down the stairs and grabbed Rexie's collar.

The knocking stopped.

Kevin released Rexie's collar. He stepped up to the door and stretched to look out the peephole. He saw a red balloon bobbing in front of the peephole. Kevin fell back just as something large slammed into the door. Kevin grabbed for Rexie who was cowering in fear.

Kevin ran up the stairs just as he heard glass shatter behind him. He looked over his shoulder and saw a white gloved hand and a polka dotted sleeved arm snaking through the side window. The fingers stretched to reach the deadbolt but it was too far to reach. The arm retracted and as Kevin reached the top of the stairs the front door exploded in a shower of wood as the dead bolt was kicked free of the doorjamb. Kevin heard the heavy metal bounce on the hardwood floor as he disappeared into his room with Rexie right behind him. He quickly slammed his door shut.

The Clown stepped into the house. He was tall, almost freakishly so, and heavy. His strength was evident even beneath the baggy polka dot clothing. He had bushy red hair that surrounded the pale white bald area at the top of his head. Even the wide smile painted over his white face could not hide the madness that was just beneath the surface. His eyes were wild and darting from side to side in search of his prey. The red balloon was tied to his finger. He slipped it off and let it float to the ceiling. He glanced around the foyer and let his eyes rise up the stairs.

Kevin struggled to push his dresser in front of his door. It was moving so slowly but finally the large wooden chest slid in front of the door. He quickly grabbed the phone and pressed the on button. There was nothing. Not a busy signal, not a tone, just silence.

"No...no...no." He whispered and looked around him. He rushed to the window and pushed it open. He could jump down but that would certainly break his legs, "Help! Someone! Help me!" He screamed as loud as he could but his only response was the turning of his bedroom door's handle. His heart leapt into his throat. He darted across the room and grabbed Rexie's collar. He pulled him into the closet. He closed the door slightly but left it open a few inches so that he could see out.

Kevin sat down with Rexie whimpering between his legs. He buried his face in his warm fur and cried softly, "Please god, please, please."

The bedroom door flew open sending the dresser crashing to the floor. The Clown stepped into the room and pushed the dresser aside with his foot. He glanced briefly at the closet door before he flipped over Kevin's bed. The Clown walked over to the window. He leaned forward to look out at the drop below.

Kevin took his chance and darted from the closet. He rushed forward and threw himself against The Clown. It felt as if he had crashed into a wall but his momentum was enough. The Clown tried to turn and grab for the window but his posture was against him and he fell through. Kevin winced when he heard the heavy body slam into the ground below.

He stepped forward and looked out the window. The Clown was lying on the grass with his neck cocked at an odd angle. Kevin could not tell if he was breathing or not, but he was not moving. Kevin almost screamed with joy when he saw a car pull to a stop at the curb. He saw his mother leap out of the car and rush towards The Clown. She stopped and looked up towards Kevin. He smiled despite the tears that were falling down his face.

Kevin felt Rexie nudging his hand. He reached down and pet his head and his neck. Everything was okay now. His hand felt wet when he pulled it away from Rexie's fur. He looked at it and saw streaks of red running down his palm. His hand began shaking as he looked down at his beloved pet.

Rexie was looking up at him with sad eyes but something was wrong. He wasn't all there. It was just his head.

"Woof."

Kevin spun around and faced the source of the bark. He was face to face with another clown, this one no taller than he was. He had blue hair and a vicious grin painted across his mouth.

"Mo-!" Kevin started to scream for his mother but the little clown leapt on top of him. They fell to the ground. Kevin landed on his back with the midget sitting on his midsection. He put a fat, meaty gloved hand over Kevin's mouth. Kevin's eyes widened in terror as the clown removed a thick hook from inside his striped jumpsuit.

Kevin tried to scream through the heavy hand.

The Little Clown looked down on him with a large toothy grin. He placed the hook to his lips, "Shhh."

Kevin shut his eyes and screamed as loud as he could.

The little clown laughed and raised the hook over his head.

What's Your Pleasure?

"Excuse me?" Jeff asked. He was sure he did not hear the old woman correctly. Certainly he didn't. She was probably close to a hundred years old, carrying a withered old cane. She was overweight and bent over at the middle of her back and was looking up at him with beady, yet oddly youthful looking brown eyes.

"What is your pleasure?" She asked again with her gravely ancient voice and it turned out that Jeff had indeed heard her correctly. He scratched his head and looked at her curiously.

"I...well I guess I'm not sure what you mean?"

They were standing on the sidewalk outside of a nondescript building. Jeff hadn't the slightest idea what might be housed inside; in fact, he barely knew where he was at all. He had taken a bus to get here, in the hopes of picking up his car, but he had taken the wrong bus entirely and now found himself in a part of town he was dangerously unfamiliar with.

"You know what I mean. Don't kid with Mother." She rubbed the bottom of her cane up the inside of Jeff's leg and tapped it against his groin, "What makes your boogsha go stiff?"

"Jesus lady!" Jeff slapped the cane away and took a step away from the old woman.

She cackled loudly.

"You no like Mother? That's fine. I have girls of all kinds for you. You like your boogsha sucked on? They do that. You can stick boogsha anywhere, they like that too."

Jeff was on the verge of laughing in the old woman's face. She was offering him girls for sex. Here was this sweet old lady, offering him girls for sex.

"Look ma'am, I'm flattered but I really don't think I need those types of services."

"You prefer boogsha to poogsha?"

"I don't know what that means."

"You like mens? Gay? Is no problem, have those as well if it's your pleasure."

"No, I'm not gay. I just don't pay for sex."

Jeff did not like to brag but he felt he was a fairly good looking man. He was about six foot tall, in reasonably good shape with shaggy brown hair, grey eyes, and a nice smile. He didn't really need to take advantage of a hooker.

"Pay money? No pay money. You keep money. Your pleasure is your payment."

Jeff couldn't tell what kind of an accent this woman was speaking in. It didn't seem familiar to him, it sounded vaguely like some kind of Slavic tongue but he could not be sure. The whole situation was too weird for him. The old woman was just an immigrant trying to survive in the city by any means necessary so he couldn't blame her for trying, even if her choice of job was a little strange. Playing barker for a whorehouse didn't seem like the most rewarding job in the world.

"Come see my girls. I have all kinds. Anything you could ever want."

Her voice seemed different. Lighter, less foreign.

"No thank you. I appreciate it. But no thank you."

"Just a peak, you have peak maybe change your mind?"

The door opened and soft violin music floated out into the street.

Jeff heard the rumbling sound of an approaching bus.

"Look, lady, thanks for the offer but no thanks. My bus is coming so – "

He was unable to finish his sentence because the woman grabbed him by the arm and with strength that seemed out of character for a woman of such an advanced age, she pulled him towards the door.

"You look!"

Jeff looked into the doorway and saw nothing but darkness. He thought for a moment that he could make out some vague shapes in the blackness but decided it was his imagination. He jerked his arm away from the woman and walked to where the bus was slowing to a stop.

"You be back boy. You will explore your desires with my girls. You wait and see."

"You're goddamned loony tunes lady. How about that? Fuck you and your girls!" Jeff climbed onto the bus.

"Oh you will." The old woman said as she watched the bus pull away, "you'll fuck us all."

She opened her black-toothed mouth and cackled.

***

It was hours before Jeff finally made it home with his newly repaired car. He was grumpy and hungry when he entered his small apartment and tossed his keys into the dish next to the door. He slammed the door shut and locked it before skulking into the living room and flopping onto the couch. He grabbed the remote and began flipping through channels. It seemed all the networks were showing old reruns. He skipped up to the pay cable channels. On the first channel there were two college girls making out. Their tongues were dancing together and their hands freely explored each other's bodies. Jeff felt a stirring in his pants. He reached down and gave himself a squeeze. He didn't have the energy to do anything about it now so he flipped the channel. The next network showed a man fucking a woman on the side of a pool table. His ass clenched with each thrust. The woman had her legs wrapped around his torso and was moaning wildly. Jeff flipped again and the screen again filled with two women going at it roughly. This time a man was furiously pounding away from behind one of the women.

"Jesus." Jeff whispered. He squeezed his crotch again and flipped off the TV. He sighed and went into his bedroom. He was too tired to jack off and was certainly too tired to cook something to eat so he decided instead to just go to bed. He peeled off his t-shirt and jeans and climbed into bed wearing nothing but his socks and boxers. He didn't even bother to climb under the covers. He was asleep moments after his head hit the pillow.

Jeff found himself standing outside the building by the bus stop. Mother was nowhere to be found and the street was empty and dark. There was a gentle wind blowing and it carried the soft violin music from the open door of the building. Jeff looked down at his body. He was wearing the smiley face boxers and white socks he went to sleep in. His body was covered with a thin sheen of sweat that caused him to feel a chill when the wind touched him.

Jeff walked towards the dark doorway. He stood on the threshold and struggled to see inside. He heard moaning from within the dark. This was different than the moaning he was used to hearing on porn films and even from his own experiences. This moaning was deeper, guttural, and primal. This was the sound of an intense pleasure, the kind of pleasure that comes from somewhere deep and untouched. This moan was joined by others until a chorus of ecstasy was filling the air around him. He felt his dick growing hard. The voices grew louder, clearly approaching a climax. Jeff felt his breath quicken as he listened to the voices. They seemed to be in unison now as if all together they were approaching an ultimate orgasm. It was now that Jeff noticed the shape in the dark. It was a woman; she had to be nude because he could make out the shape of her body perfectly. Even in the darkness, he could tell it was flawless. Jeff felt his mouth fill with saliva. His dick twitched with desire. He wanted that woman. He thought for a moment that he heard himself growl, but that was impossible. Why would he growl? Jeff wanted to step into that door more than anything else.

A supple white hand emerged from the dark. Its fingertips were capped with bright red nails. The hand brushed his cheek and then dragged the tip of the bright red fingernail down his hard moist chest. A thin trail of blood marked the trail of the finger. Jeff winced slightly. The hand moved away and disappeared into the dark door.

The moaning was reaching its crescendo.

"Jeff…" A soft voice whispered, "What is your pleasure?"

Jeff shook his head slightly. His eyelids fluttered and he fell backwards.

***

Jeff snapped awake and cracked his head against something hard. He opened his eyes and realized he was sitting in the driver's seat of his car. He was dressed in his boxers and socks. He looked outside the window he had just bumped his head against and found that he was parked outside the building he had just been dreaming about.

"What the fuck..." Jeff slammed the car in gear and sped off. He didn't notice the thin trail of blood on his chest until the next morning.

This continued for seven weeks. Each night, Jeff would go to sleep and dream of the building. Each time he would wake up in his car parked across from it. As time progressed, he found himself waking up outside the car and closer and closer to the building.

Finally, he awoke with his hand on the door handle ready to twist and pull the door open. He didn't understand what was happening to him or why he was sleep-driving himself to a whorehouse on the other side of the city. It was beginning to affect his work. He was unable to concentrate on anything longer than a few minutes before his thoughts drifted back to the building. Jeff had lost control of himself and this terrified him.

It was mid-way through the eighth week that he decided to visit the building. He felt as if he had no choice but to go. His life was no longer his own and he needed to speak with that old woman to get her to undo whatever that she had done to him.

He went the very next morning. Jeff parked his car across the street and sat for a few minutes just watching the building. No one went in and no one came out. The old woman was nowhere to be seen. He scratched his chest absently. That cut had never healed quite right. He had spent weeks struggling with how to explain the cut on his chest and eventually factored it to some kind of psychosomatic hysterical reaction to the dreams.

So he forced himself to climb out of his car and cross the street. He quickly stepped over the sidewalk and reached for the door.

"Ah. You come back."

Jeff spun around quickly and felt his heart leaping into his throat. The old woman was standing behind him. She was leaning on her cane and grinning her black toothed grin at him. Suddenly, Jeff thought he should do nothing else besides run back to his car and get the fuck out of Dodge.

"You stay away longer than the others. I proud of you; that mean you strong. In the end it always brings you back."

"What are you talking about?"

"Your boogsha. The boogsha always brings the men folk back." She smiled gently and for a moment Jeff forgot she was an ancient old woman, "Go on inside. It be time now."

Even though every fiber of his being was screaming at him to run away, Jeff obeyed.

He pulled open the door and was not greeted by the impenetrable darkness he was expecting. Instead, he was greeted by a soft red light that illuminated the long hallway ahead of him. He stepped inside and the door closed behind him. He thought it was rather cliché to have red lighting in a sex den or whorehouse or whatever this place was. The floor beneath his feet was soft, almost liquid like. He thought he heard squishing with each step but could not be sure. His hearing was mostly filled with the soft groaning of the other patrons. He tried to look into the rooms as he passed them. He could only make out vague pulsating shapes through thresholds. None of the rooms had doors or curtains. Only the darkness of the rooms provided privacy. Jeff heard someone call out for Jesus. Curiously, it was hard to determine whether that yell was in pleasure or in fear.

Jeff felt the hairs on the back of his neck stand on end. He spun around quickly and found himself face to face with the most beautiful woman he had ever seen. She had golden hair that fell in curls to her shoulders. Her eyes gleamed with a deep cool blue that made the clearest ocean look like mud. Her nude body was as hard and perfect as a sculpture.

Jeff opened his mouth to speak but she held a blood red nail-tipped finger to her red lips. She then took Jeff's hand and placed it against her breast.

Jeff felt his knees weaken and his mouth filled with water.

"Do you desire me?" Her voice was soft and smooth, as flawless as her body.

Jeff simply nodded, fearing that if he spoke, his drool would spill out of his mouth.

"Speak it." She said, "Tell me of your desire."

Jeff took in her beauty. She released his hand and he gently caressed her smooth skin. He ran his fingers across her stomach and over her hip.

His eyes were unable to see the other side of her body. He was too fascinated with the perfection of the front of her to be worried about the back. He would not see the dripping skinless flesh that covered her back, nor the thick leathery tail that twitched at the base of her spine.

"Do you desire me, Jeff?" She asked again.

"Yes." He said. His voice was thick with his wanting, his pants straining with his need.

She took a step forward and pressed herself against him, "Do you wish to taste me?" She did not wait for an answer. She pressed her mouth against his and kissed him deeply.

Jeff felt her tongue slide into his mouth. It slid deeper, deeper, and deeper still. It brushed against his uvula causing him to buck and gag. Still it slid deeper down his throat. He could feel it slithering into his chest. She pulled her head back revealing the thick rigid flesh. She smiled as the tongue plunged further into him.

Jeff's eyes widened as his airway was cut off. He looked down at the tongue as it pulsated and shifted. His survival instinct took over and he bit down on the flesh. Thick black liquid exploded from the tongue and spilled over his chest and into his mouth. The woman fell back as her tongue ripped apart. The half inside Jeff's body slithered its way through his mouth and down into his guts. He gasped for air and immediately fell to his knees as vomit exploded from his mouth.

His brain was making the obvious statement that Jeff had made a very bad mistake. He staggered to his feet and looked at the woman standing before him. Her formally pristine skin was now covered in the black goo that spilled from her tongue. She had her head tilted and a smile on her face. She raised her hand and Jeff felt his body go rigid. Her mouth opened and the stubby tongue slipped past her lips, spilling more of the black goo over her chin. She chuckled and pushed her hand forward.

Jeff felt his body flying through the air. The long hall blew past him, its walls changing from soft drywall and passion-filled doorways, to hard rock and scream-filled corridors. He stopped and was hanging in mid-air. He heard shuffling behind him and strained to look over his shoulder. All he could see was a large wooden cross being raised. The cross had large gore covered spikes running along its wooden arms and leg.

"Jesus fuck…" He whispered and began squirming. He struggled to get free of whatever force was holding him in the air, "Help me! GOD HELP ME!" His voice echoed in the cave like chamber and each echo sounded more and more like he was mocking himself. He saw the naked woman step into the room. She still had her arm up and she twisted her wrist to move Jeff into position.

"No…please…"

She pushed her hand forward roughly and Jeff shot backwards. He felt the spikes pierce his arms and legs. He looked down and watched as the tips burst through the other sides of his arms spilling his flesh and blood on the floor. He noticed now that the floor was slick with bile and gore. He could no longer tell which was his own.

A wire slipped out of the tip of the spikes and wrapped around him holding him tight around the cross. Jeff moaned as he felt the wire digging into his flesh. He had come here for pleasure and now he could feel nothing but pain. He surveyed the damage, even as he felt his head growing light and his vision blurred. He had spikes going through the length of his arms which were both stretched out across the T of the cross. His legs were tightly bound together with spikes stuck through his calves and thighs. He looked down at his chest and saw the spikes had broken through his torso just as the wiring had. He could feel the cool metal against his insides.

The woman climbed up his body and stared into his eyes.

"Why…" he muttered.

The woman said nothing. She simply opened her mouth and licked his face with her stump of a tongue. Jeff barely felt the rough tongue cross his cheek before he succumbed to the peaceful, painless blackness that awaited him.

He didn't know how long he was out but as soon as his eyelids fluttered he was overcome with a pain so strong that it almost knocked him unconscious again. He managed to stay awake however and noticed that he was alone in a cavern. He did hear a clicking noise growing louder. He knew what that was. It was HER. She was coming. Her cane clicked against the rough stone floor and she stepped into the open cavern. She looked up at Jeff, her eyes were bright and her face was filled with a look of smug satisfaction.

"I have waited 2000 years for this moment." She said.

"Let me go you old cow." Jeff whispered. It hurt to talk.

"It's such a shame. You don't even know what you are." She clacked her way in a circle around the cross, "Nice and tight." She reached up with her cane and slammed it against his leg.

Jeff howled in pain, "You fucking bitch! God forgive me! Please free me from this hell!" He was crying now.

"You aren't in Hell, boy. Not by a long shot." When she crossed back into Jeff's vision she was fully nude. The folds of her old wrinkled skin fell in waves. Her breasts dangled to her waist like limp hoses. She was walking differently though. She had tossed her cane away. Jeff had heard it clatter against the stones. Every step she took seemed to cause her skin to tighten. The grey curls that sat on her head began to stretch out and darken. Her hair turned a deep black and fell in waves down her back. The wrinkles on her skin faded away and her body became svelte and tight. This was a different woman entirely, but a woman that seemed familiar to Jeff. He could not be sure why but it was a carnal recognition.

"All I had was time, the endless waiting. The ground beneath you is slick with the flesh and blood of the men that came before you. But you, you are the last one."

Jeff was sure he was hallucinating. He was being tortured by some black blooded bitch and had lost his mind and was imagining this hideous old crone turning into a beautiful young woman before his eyes. Maybe all of this was a dream. Maybe he was back home in his bed sleeping and dreaming this whole thing.

"You are not dreaming, Jeff. "

That caused Jeff to release his bladder. The piss streaming down his leg sent fresh pain throughout his body. He closed his eyes to fight off the waves of nausea that passed over him. When he opened them again, Mother's face was inches from his own. This was no small feat because he figured he was hanging 10 – 15 feet off the ground. He looked down and noticed that the entire lower half of her body had changed into a snake.

"Oh God."

She clicked her tongue, "God, Jesus, you keep saying those names like one of them will swoop down and save you." The woman grabbed his face and held it steady, "God and Jesus are the reason you are here!" She slapped his face and cackled, rocking back on her massive snake tail.

Jeff was convinced now that he had gone completely insane; still, he wanted to know just how far this madness was going to go.

"Who are you?" He asked.

The snake woman slithered around the cavern and wrapped her arms around him from behind, "I am the first. I am Mother, the true wife of Adam."

"EVE?" Jeff asked incredulously. He was rewarded with another slap.

"I came before the whore, Eve. It should be my name in the books: Lilith is the true mother of Eden. Instead, I am banished and that sow took my place. I do prefer the name Lamia to be quite honest." She stroked his cheek, "Do you know what Lamia has been known as?"

"No." Jeff sighed; he could feel his strength draining from his body.

"Child killer." Lamia said cheerfully, "but no one really understood that. I wasn't killing children indiscriminately. I did have a reason." She slithered around the cross and let her tail coil around her. She rested in it as if it was a throne.

"I'm dying…" Jeff whispered.

"Yes, but don't you want to know why?"

"Because some demon girl strapped me to a cross?"

"She wasn't a demon. She was what your filthy species was before you became what you are today."

"Neat." Jeff's head dropped. He was simply too exhausted to argue. Lamia lurched forward and slapped him hard across the face.

"Not yet. We're not finished." She returned to her throne, "I want you going to Him knowing why."

Jeff looked at her. She moved forward and ran her finger under his lip. She held it up before his eyes. There was a thick glob of blood trickling down her finger.

"This is what it is all about, blood; blood and vengeance." She placed the finger into her mouth and sucked the blood from its tip, "All the thousands I have brought here and slaughtered, all for blood and vengeance. It is his blood and my vengeance. Today it finally ends and I can be at peace."

"His blood?" Jeff didn't understand.

"Yes, it is the Blood of the Lamb, Jesu, of Yahweh, the blood of Jeff." She giggled.

"Are you saying I'm Jesus?"

Lamia laughed.

"No. I am saying you're related." She said, "But you are the last of them; the end of the road. The Holy Bloodline, the Blood of God and Jesus ends with you. All the thousands and thousands I have devoured has lead up to you: The last living heir of the Creator."

Lamia lurched forward and shot her hand through Jeff's pants. He felt her grab the entirety of his manhood in her grip.

"You'll hang here and bleed to death like the Son did. It's unfortunate I do not have a spear to speed up the process." She jerked her arm and with it, ripped his genitalia from his body.

Jeff screamed in agony. His vision went white as the pain ripped through his being. He felt blood pouring from the gaping wound in his groin.

Lamia cackled insanely. She lowered herself and let Jeff's lifeblood wash over her face.

Jeff felt his life seeping away. The pain was gone now. He had no reaction when Lamia moved within inches of his face. He could smell his blood on her skin. She held his manhood up to his face.

"What is your pleasure?" She asked.

Jeff had no answer.

The Strange Tale of Griffin Shard

One

"Tell me something, Mr. Rufio. Do you fear a god?" The old man asked with his weak voice.

Mr. Rufio, Reginald Rufio as it were, sat down in a chair next to the old man's bed. He folded his hands in his lap and let his eyes rest on the smoldering fire on the opposite side of the room. He was not prepared for existentialist conversation, certainly not with an old heathen who was surely breathing the last of his breaths.

"I asked you a question Mr. Rufio. I do not believe I have much time for you to ponder it."

"I'm here to witness your death, Doctor. I really have no interest in discussing my religious intent."

"You have sat in that chair every evening, night, and dawn

for the past seven weeks. Surely, you have at least a mild desire to converse rather than sit and watch a dying fire until the sun breaks?"

"I can assure you I do not."

The doctor scoffs and lets out a bark of a cough. From the corner of his eye, Rufio notices a red glob arching through the air. It lands silently on the old man's quilt.

"Less in than out nowadays I think." The old doctor wipes a string of blood from his mouth. "Not long now, Mr. Rufio. I hope you've earned your money well watching me die."

"It would do us both better if you died in silence."

"Am I not allowed my final words before I am claimed? Am I to be denied my dying proclamation? Surely not. I am a god fearing man, Mr. Rufio; perhaps I am inclined to confess."

"The god you fear is the lord of darkness and I am not a man of the cloth. I cannot hear your confession and by god I would refuse it if I were."

The old doctor lurched forward and grabbed Rufio's arm with a vice like grip. Surprising, considering his fingers looked as if they'd shatter at the lightest touch.

"My god is the one true god. I fear him as you fear your own, as your own fears him, and you will hear my confession, Rufio." He squeezed tighter, "You will hear and you will listen."

Rufio felt a chill in his bones and did his best to remain calm. He looked the old doctor in the eyes and what he saw there was life. They were not the eyes of a dying man. They were clear and bright. Still, Rufio hid his shock and spoke. "Remove your hand from my coat. I shall have to have it burned to rid the taint your touch leaves."

The old man laughed, "Such an insult." His voice seemed clearer, stronger, "In the desk on your right, you shall find parchment and ink. You will need it to record my confession."

"I will do no such thing. Your time for confession is past. You have been tried and convicted and will die without the last rites and buried in unconsecrated ground."

"Yes, well, in the meantime, you will write down what I tell you or by my god you will not survive the night."

It was now Rufio's turn to scoff. "I have nothing to fear from you old man. My soul is protected and I am a righteous man."

"Believe what you will, Mr. Rufio." The old man rested his head on his pillow. He supposed he should be grateful to his condemners for allowing him to die in his own bed. He had a warm hearth, food brought to him regularly, and good company morning, noon, and night. This company was forbidden to speak to him and was there simply to watch him die, but he had managed to get them all to speak with him occasionally. Except Mr. Rufio, until tonight. He knew that Rufio was a pious man, which was exactly why he wanted to confess to him. Partially, so that the world could understand his crimes, but more so to see this normally kind man driven mad by the hearing of them. "They accused me of many things, Rufio, many terrible things. Aren't you the least curious to understand why? Even to know if these charges are true?"

"Not if my life depended on the knowing or on the understanding. Thou shalt not suffer a demon to speak. Thou shalt not suffer me to listen."

"Oh poppycock, I've heard enough nonsense from you. I have studied religion and gods decades before you were fiddled with by your priest. The knowledge I have in my heathen brain is enough to bring the church to its knees."

"How dare you insinuate…"

"Oh do shut up, Rufio. Your indignation is sure to hasten my demise and I have plenty to speak before I go."

Rufio jumped from his chair. "I will not stand for this any longer. Gold is not enough by far to listen to your blasphemy." He walked towards the door. As he approached he felt his body lurch and rise into the air. He crashed heavily against the heavy oak door and slid to the ground. His vision blurred and his head spun.

"Hours and hours left to go and so much knowledge for you to know." The doctor chuckled, "Grab your parchment and ink dear Rufio for I have a story to tell."

"I shan't listen." Rufio whispered.

"Oh, but you shall." The old man beckoned with his fingers and Rufio began to slide along the floor. With a cackle the man jerked his arm and Rufio flew into the air. He fell hard against the chair. He winced as a nail point tore into his forehead.

"What magic is this?" Rufio cried.

"There is no such thing as magic, Rufio. Only power," The old man's eyes turned a red only describable as burning blood and his voice changed to a demonic din, "unfathomable power!"

Rufio felt as if his mind were shattering. When he saw the old man's eyes he could take no more. His own eyes rolled back in his head and he fell into darkness.

***

Rufio's eyes opened slowly. His head was throbbing and a wave of nausea washed over him when he tried to move.

"It's about time you woke. Your stench is not pleasant."

Rufio began to protest but caught sight of the dark stain on the front of his trousers. He had soiled himself. "I must go at once to a doctor. I have had some kind of spell."

"You've had a fright, that's all. Run home and take care of yourself. Return here on the hour and we shall begin."

"Nonsense, I'm bleeding."

"Yes, quite profusely. We certainly can't have you losing blood now can we? You're going to need that. Hurry now. The night grows long and we haven't much time."

"I beg your pardon but I am not wont to heed to your schedule. I shall go to the doctor and return on my next shift. You're not likely to expire this night, this town should be so lucky."

"I'll not tell you again, Rufio. You will return here on the hour or I shall peel the skin from your daughter's body and dance a jig with it on the grave of your beloved Clara!"

"My Clara is not dead you fool and I will ring your neck until your eyes go purple if you even mention my daughter again."

"She lives for as long as I allow it: On the hour."

"You are a monster the likes of which has not walked this earth."

"Look in my eyes and heed my words, Rufio. On the hour or else. You'd do well not to try me." He twisted his hand and the heavy oak door opened with a bang, "On. The. Hour. Now take your leave. Your stench is dizzying."

Rufio took his leave.

Two

Fear is a terrible thing and it followed Rufio all the way home. He feared for his young daughter and for his beautiful wife. He feared his own mind, a near certainty that he is caught in some kind of fever dream and fit of madness. He touched his forehead as he crossed the cobble stone street and his fingers came away wet with blood. He winced slightly from the burning pain that accompanied his touch. Surely then he wasn't dreaming. That meant that he must be mad. That old man could not wield such power. It was the stuff of fairytales, malarkey and prattle that had no validity in the real world. Still though his fear followed and clawed ever deeper into his gut. Would he test the old man? Would he risk his family by ignoring his commands?

Rufio did not believe there would be much harm in adhering to the man's wish. He would listen and take the confession. It was not worth the risk of the slightest harm to his family. All the old man wants is to speak his mind. Rufio decided he would listen and write down the vile words the old man spoke. He would do this for his family and because he believed God would smile down upon him for hearing the words of a condemned man.

Satisfied, Rufio rushed home.

***

The hour was late and Rufio was careful not to make too much noise as he changed his clothes. His wife was snoring softly and did not wake as he changed. He kissed her gently on the forehead and slipped from the room. He paused at his daughter's door and pushed it open slowly. He saw her shape wrapped up in blankets. He walked over to her bedside and gently pulled the blanket from her head.

He didn't immediately notice her flesh was missing. It wasn't until he pulled the blanket down past her chin that he saw the gristle and bone of her jaw and the wetness of the muscles twinkling in the moonlight.

"Dear God!" He shouted. The skinless face of his daughter turned to him, teeth gleaming and wide.

"What's wrong, Daddy?" She asked.

Rufio staggered back and fell against the wall. He hid his face in horror and agony. He heard her slide from the bed and that slight peeling sound as her bare, skinless feet stepped across the wooden floor. He could almost see the bloody footprints in his mind's eye and the thought nearly drove him mad.

"Are you okay, Daddy?"

Rufio opened his eyes. His daughter stood before him with a curious look on her face, her beautiful face. He had imagined it all. He placed his hand on her cheek.

"I…I'm sorry for waking you. I had a start that's all. Let's get you back into bed."

She smiled that smile that always warmed his heart and climbed back into her bed. Rufio kissed her and covered her with the blanket.

"Are you going back to the bad man?" She asked.

Rufio tucked the blanket under her chin, "Yes. I will see you in the morning. Sweet dreams my sweet, Alouisa."

She closed her eyes and Rufio slipped from the room. He pulled the door closed and rested his burning head against the cool wood. Never had he had such a fright and his heart was only now beginning to slow. He knew then if that old man made any attempt to harm his daughter that he would rip him apart limb from limb and knew that God would smile down upon him as he did so.

***

The walk back was rather stressful for Rufio. Despite his vow, he was still incredibly shaken by the vision of his daughter stripped of her skin. He rubbed at his head and winced in pain as his fingers brushed against his wound. It was a miracle that Alouisa had not noticed it. She would have been frightened to see her father hurt. But, luck at that moment was on Rufio's side and she did not see. After tucking her in, he quickly gathered the supplies he was ordered to bring and set himself back to the run-down old mansion that was holding a man most foul. He arrived on the doorstep just as the bell began to chime the hour. He quickly stepped inside and locked the door behind him. He heard the old man hacking away upstairs.

"Just made it eh, Rufio?" The man laughed.

Rufio scowled and climbed the stairs to the old man's bed chambers. He entered and pushed the door closed behind him.

"Did you get it all?"

"I did." Rufio answered.

"Good. Leave the parchment on the desk. Bring the quill and inkwell to me."

Rufio complied. He handed the quill and ink to the old man.

"Kneel down here. Closer you fool."

Rufio obeyed and knelt closer to the bed. He knew the man was frail and despite the earlier events he did not think the man could do much damage. He realized how foolish this assumption was when the old man swiftly jabbed the quill into the wound on Rufio's forehead. He felt the sharp edge dig into his skin and scrape against his skull. His eyes welled with tears and he cried out in pain. He tried to pull away but the man clamped his hand on the back of Rufio's head. It felt like a vice grip and he was unable to pull away.

"Calm yourself. You're mewling like a newborn calf. It won't be but a moment or two more."

But Rufio could not be calmed. He could feel a strange sucking sensation where the quill had entered his flesh. Finally, the man shoved him away. He turned over the inkwell and dumped its contents to the floor. He placed the tip of the quill against the lip of the well and Rufio watched in horror as his blood streamed forth to fill the inkwell.

"God in Heaven, this is witchery!" He gasped.

"It may very well be. But I am no witch." The man held out the quill and ink well to Rufio, "Shall we begin?"

Three

Rufio held the quill in his shaking hand. The tips of his fingers felt as if they were on fire.

"I'll start with my name, since you have yet to ask it, despite your time here."

"I do not wish to know…"

Rufio winced as a wave of pain shot through his fingers.

"Do not be so rude, Rufio. It is unbecoming, as I was saying… My name is Griffin Shard. I am a man of modest wealth, nearly entirely ill-gotten. I have prospered on the misery of others. You see, I practice a very particular trade, one that I am singular in, at least in this part of the world. Why aren't you writing, Rufio?"

In fact, it was taking every square ounce of will on his behalf to keep the quill from scratching across the parchment. Sweat was beading on his forehead and his face was contorted in pain. He was convinced this writing tool had taken on a life of its own.

"You are quite right in that, Rufio. You gave it life with your blood. Fighting it will only cause your discomfort to increase. Allow the tool to do its work."

Rufio closed his eyes and gave up fighting. His hand was now in the command of this quill and it quickly filled the parchment with thick red letters matching word for word the sentences Shard had spoken moments ago.

"It remembers quite well." Shard said with a slight chuckle, "Shall I continue?"

Rufio lowered his head, "Yes, you bastard. Continue and finish your cursed tale quickly."

Shard relaxed in his bed and let his eyes drift up towards the ceiling, "It began with stones. You see, when I was a child I ran across an old gypsy woman and she told me of the magicks, the old magicks, held deep within the earth. Magicks that can be accessed if one is able to find stones old enough. That knowledge took hold of my young imagination; years later I left my home, what was left of it after raiders destroyed it that is. I left in search of these magicks. I would not rest until I found them."

"There haven't been raiders in these parts for centuries. You are mad as a hatter."

Shard cast a deep, horrifying look at Rufio. He had grown tired of these interruptions and Rufio was at once chilled to the bone. He was also entirely convinced that this story was true which meant that this old man before him was hundreds of years old. What sort of pact with the Devil had Shard made to live so long?

Shard took a deep breath and let out another monstrous cough. This shook his body violently and when the cough finally subsided, there was a string of blood running from his nostril.

He wiped the fluid away with sad smile, "Even with all my magicks, time is a most vicious bitch. The most vicious of all I think." He gave a heavy sigh and continued, "It was the stones that set me on course to become what I am today. I found the first in a cave outside of Shrevedon."

Rufio had never even heard of this village.

"The others I found scattered throughout the corners of the Earth. Dark places, light places, holy lands, and most especially unholy ones. The stones drew dark forces, you see, they were not tools of a righteous man. They are a dark power. I had collected hundreds of them before I discovered how to truly harness their gifts. It took a dark man in the north of Africa before I would know."

"What do you mean it took a dark man?"

"It took his blood. It took his knowledge. I needed what only he knew and he refused to tell me. I learned, in my travels through those lands, of only one way to obtain the knowledge that another will not willingly relinquish."

Rufio was quite sure he did not want to know that method but again was sure he would know in short time.

"It was no easy task to kidnap the man. He was an ancient man to be sure but he was powerful. It nearly cost me my life, but in the end I succeeded."

"Dear God…" Rufio whispered fearfully, "What did you do to him?"

"I killed him and beneath the largest brightest moon I ever laid eyes on, I ate him."

Rufio paled.

"I ate until I was full and then I ate some more. I drank his blood like the Vampires of old and devoured his flesh like the beasts that circled us. I split open his chest and ate his heart first for that is the core and the home to the soul. It was still warm when I took my first bite and, truth be told, it beat twice more after I swallowed. It was delectable. I ate his brains last; they were cold. I left the remains for the creatures patiently waiting in the night."

Rufio saw the hunger in the man's eyes and the quill wrote on.

"The knowledge wasn't instantaneous. Of course, I had to digest the man. Strangely enough, I never defecated after I ate him. My body absorbed every ounce of him. There would be no waste at all. Come to think of it, there never was."

"You are a devil." Rufio said, "A devourer of human flesh, a fiend!"

"Yes, I am all of these things. I ate for knowledge, I learned so much from so many. I learned from men. I learned from women. I learned from Heads of State and from gutter trash. I learned from the old and I learned from the very, very young."

Rufio's eyes widened, "You... ate children?"

"Yes, frequently. It was not only knowledge I was obtaining from these people. It was life. I had passed my first century by half and did not look a day beyond my thirtieth. It took another dozen years before I knew exactly what was granting me this longevity and now that I knew this I could harness it. I had learned the secrets of the ancient stones from the African and from that, had great magicks at my disposal. I know now that it wasn't the power I was after. It was the darkness. It called to me. Caressed me, welcomed me. I could wipe out a village with a thought but that was not enough. I wanted to know the source. I visited your churches and watched you fools falling on your knees wailing at the skies. I admired the madness for a time despite knowing the truth."

"What truth do you think you know? You are nothing but a vessel of evil; a monster that murders innocents and eats their flesh like some kind of rabid dog!"

"Dear Rufio, do brace yourself for the truth you are about to learn. It will come as a shock to you." Shard shifted his weight and leaned towards Rufio. The smell of death wafted from him and Rufio had to fight off his sickness, "Your god is dead, slain a thousand years ago."

"Blasphemy!"

"Perhaps to some, but truth to others. It was my God, my dark l
ord who devoured yours; devoured him just as I had devoured so
many."

A look of pure pleasure washed over him. He was lost in a
memory that filled him with such bliss that for a moment Rufio
feared he would not return from it. Rufio had never seen such
happiness on a man's face. It was almost chilling.

"I know this to be true, Mr. Rufio. Unequivocally so, irrefutably."

"What is it that convinces you so?"

Shard looked Rufio in the eye with his steel frigid stare.

"I know this because I met my God. I met him and he
told me."

Four

Rufio read the words that had scrawled across the parchment.
This was surely more madness spewing from the vile mouth of
this Griffin Shard. God was almighty. He could not be killed and
certainly not by whatever dark master Shard worshipped.

"It is true, Rufio. I do apologize for having to be the one to tell
you. Your God is dead and mine has taken his place.

"I have endured your blasphemy far too long. This madness is
over." Rufio flung the quill from his hand. It stopped in mid-air.

"I shall be the one to tell you when this madness is at its end,
Rufio."

Shard twitched his hand and the quill flew back towards Rufio.
It pierced through the back of his hand and forced itself through
until the tip burst from his palm.

Rufio howled in pain and grabbed his wrist.

"Keep writing, Rufio."

Tears were streaming down Rufio's face. The quill twitched

and began mobbing across the parchment. Rufio wept in pain as the quill moved in his hand.

"The Father of Lies they call him. He has set his children on their paths. I have served him well and for my dedication I was rewarded with great power. There are others, some much older, some pre-human. There is even a woman out there who kills in the name of vengeance. She does not even realize that she is killing for him." Shard laughs, "She has taken it upon herself to end the Holy Bloodline, difficult work that is."

"My hunger took me all across this world. At last I settled here. My only regret is that I did not have better control over my… needs. I was discovered and here I lay now awaiting death to claim me. I have lived a hundred lives, Rufio, and to be honest, I am not quite ready for that to end."

Rufio was in too much pain to respond.

Shard leaned forward and ripped the quill out of his hand. Rufio shrieked in pain.

"I have picked up many skills in my lifetime." Shard grabbed Rufio's hand and held it tightly between his palms. Rufio felt a searing heat spread over his hand. Shard released him and his hand was healed.

"I can give life just as quickly as I can take it away." Shard leaned back in his bed, "There is another gift I possess. It is perhaps my greatest gift and the one that has proven to be the most useful in all my years."

Rufio rubbed his hand, "Then perhaps you should get one last use of it before death comes to take you back to your master!"

"Why thank you for that permission, Mr. Rufio. You are a most accommodating man."

Shard launched himself forward and locked his hands around

Rufio's head with a vice like grip. Rufio tried to push him off but this frail old man was too powerful.

"This shall not hurt a bit." Shard hissed.

Rufio could not answer. The world seemed to melt away around him. His body shook once and he succumbed to the coming black.

***

His daughter was waiting for him when Rufio arrived home a short time later.

She smiled up at him lovingly and he patted her on the head. He returned her smile.

"You should be in bed." He said.

"I wanted to wait for you." Alouisa said.

"Very well, you've waited and I am home now. Off to bed. It will be morning quite soon."

Alouisa ran to him and hugged him tightly, "I love you."

"And I you."

She walked towards the stairs, "Good night, Father."

"Good night, Alicia."

Alouisa paused at the stairs for a moment. Had he called her the wrong name? It was very late perhaps she was tired and misheard or perhaps he was tired and misspoke.

"Alouisa, off to bed!" Rufio called.

She nodded and trotted up stairs.

***

Griffin Shard awoke with a cough. He wiped a blob of blood from his lips and looked at it curiously. He heard something rustling next to him and turned to see a young man sitting in the chair next to his bed.

"Who are you?" Shard asked.

The young man, barely past being a boy, looked at him with fear in his eyes.

"I am not to speak to you."

"Don't be silly. I am a gentleman and you would be rude to decline speaking with me."

Shard looked around the room.

"Why am I..." He looked down at his bed clothes, at his old wrinkled hands, "Dear God!"

The young man jumped from his chair and backed away from the bed.

"What has he done to me?" Shard screamed, "You! Boy! Help me! What has he done??!!"

"Pl-please sir. Calm yourself."

"You do not understand. I am Reginald Rufio! He has stolen my body!"

There was madness in his eyes that terrified the young man. This was his first shift watching the dying man and he had not been properly prepared for such an outburst.

"Please! Please help me!"

The young man fled.

Rufio howled in misery and flung back the blanket. His bare legs were brittle and riddled with sores. He attempted to move his legs but they would not budge.

"MY FAMILY! SHARD, YOU BASTARD!"

The tears would not cease and his heart shattered. The old body could not take the stress of this pain. He screamed out the name of his wife and of his daughter and as these words passed his lips, the last breath of life passed with him.

***

Rufio stepped into the dark bedroom and began to undress. Inside, he himself knew his name. No one would ever know the truth. He tilted his head for a moment; almost sure he could hear some deep howl from a distance.

"Reginald?" His wife had awakened.

"Yes, my dear." Rufio removed the remainder of his clothing and climbed into bed with his wife, "Good morning my love. I've missed you."

He placed his hand on her face and kissed her, "Oh yes. How I have missed you."

Looking Glass

So she stood.

In front of the mirror. Her short cropped lavender hair moist with sweat. A single bang floating down over her eyes.

"I hate you." She says to the reflection.

"But I love you." The reflection answers back. The lavender hair, the thick mascara, the smeared lipstick.

"I don't give a fuck. I hate you and I will always hate you and I don't give a fuck what you think!"

The reflection lowers her head and begins to cry.

"I'm sorry." The reflection says, "I am so sorry for what you feel."

"You don't know what love is. You don't understand it." She says.

"But I do...I swear that I do."

"You don't." She reaches forward, caressing the reflection. The soft wet eyes, the pale pink cheeks.

"Love is getting lost and not caring." the reflection says.

"Love is a cliché." She says.

"Love is not letting go for anything."

"Love is dying inside."

The reflection reaches forward and touches her hand.

"Love is opening your soul..."

"or a vein." She says.

She traces her finger along the jaw line of the reflection, across the dry lips, the long neck.

"It isn't about pain." The reflection whispers.

"But that's all it is."

She folds her fingers into a fist. Tight, rock like.

"I love you." The reflection whispers.

"I hate you so much." She cries softly, "Let me hate you."

The reflection falls silent.

She slams her fist into the glass.

The world crumbles.

She cries and the reflection lies in pieces.

"I love you." The reflections whisper, a thousand voices at once, "You can shatter me into a million pieces and I will love you."

She looks down into the reflections. She looks down into her selves.

"Why do I hate you?" She asks her selves, "Why do I hate you?"

The reflections are silent.

They have no answer, for they do not know.

She cries. She cries and cries until the reflections are lost in a sea of black. She cries and she wonders.

She has no answer. For she does not know.

Interrogation

"Tell me the truth now. Tell me what you saw."

"I saw a dark place."

The sheriff leaned back in his seat, the leather of his thick belt creaked. He looked across the table at the young girl. She couldn't have been more than sixteen. Her eyes were heavily shadowed both from makeup and the bags she carried beneath them. Her hair was black but the roots were growing in blonde. She looked back at him with her red blue eyes and for just a moment she looked skeletal.

"What do you mean a dark place?" he asked.

"It was like there was no light," She sniffled and wiped her eyes with the back of her hand, looking even younger as she did, "there was something there, I know there was but all I could see was… was dark. There had to be something right? Those people… what happened… something had to do that." She was weeping now.

The sheriff clasped his hands together and rested them on the old table. He had a gold watch on his wrist that gleamed even in the dim light in the interview room.

"The lights were on when we arrived," he said, "did you turn them on after it all went dark?"

"What? No. You don't understand. The lights were never off."

"You said it was dark."

She shook her head, "No. A dark place, like a dark… shape or something."

"Another person?"

"I don't know. I don't know what it was. Just that it was there and it ripped them apart."

"So you saw it happen?"

"I just saw the dark and the… the pieces." She glanced down towards her feet, "The blood washed over my shoes. They're ruined." She whispered.

"We'll call your parents and have them bring you clothes to change into."

The girl nodded her head.

The sheriff looked towards the door. One of his deputies was standing outside waving at him. He stood and walked to the door. He pulled the door open and stepped out.

"The Fed is here." The deputy gestured over his shoulder.

"Keep an eye on her." The sheriff patted his deputy on the shoulder and walked down the hall.

The federal agent that was patiently waiting in the sheriff's office was not a federal agent at all. At least not in the way the deputy thought. His name was Jack Carter. He sat contentedly in the sheriff's chair puffing on a cigarette. The case file was open on the desk before him. He held his cigarette between his lips and thumbed through the crime scene photos.

The photos showed a gruesome scene. There didn't appear to be a body intact at all, just pieces, parts, and chunks scattered around a gore-covered room.

Jack set the photos aside and quickly scanned the crime scene report. The incident happened at a small club on the outskirts of the town. Thursday night at nine o'clock so the place wasn't as crowded as it would have been on a weekend. The report listed a suspected number of twelve dead and one unharmed survivor. The sheriff's report described this as "interesting."

The report described the scene as a "sea of blood." As Jack read on, his eyebrow arched slightly. His reading was interrupted when the office door burst open.

"You wanna tell me just what in hell you think you are doing?" the sheriff shouted, "Put that goddamn cigarette out and get out of my fucking chair!"

Jack glanced around for an ashtray, and not finding one; he licked his fingers and crushed the edge of the stick. He dropped the butt and ash into the trash.

"You must be Sheriff Paul," Jack stated as he stood up, "Sheriff James Paul?"

Sheriff Paul nodded and scowled at Jack, "We don't need federal involvement here."

Jack stepped around the desk, "No, of course not."

The sheriff pushed past Jack and sat in his chair. He folded his hands together and rested them on the desk, "I'm a little confused as to how you even found out about this."

"Of course." Jack sat in a chair across from the sheriff.

"You inclined to fill me in?"

"No." Jack locked eyes with the Sheriff, "Look, James…"

"Sheriff will be fine."

"Sheriff James, you have quite a tragedy on your hands. Small town like this certainly cannot have the resources to solve such a… unique situation."

"It seems to me this isn't such a 'unique situation' as you described." The sheriff reached into his desk and removed to files, "Seems to me that this has happened over in Georgia a month ago and in Mississippi just a week and one day ago. Now it happened here in my town in the great state of Texas. Us small town cops can get a lot accomplished in a few hours."

Jack nodded slightly.

"See I spoke to these other departments and they both mentioned some mysterious federal agent swooping in to check things out. Thing is the F.B.I. doesn't know who he is and he has a habit of vanishing before any questions can be asked."

"I'm not with the F.B.I. so they would not have any knowledge of me."

"What type of fed are you exactly?"

Jack smiled, "I'd like to speak with your witness."

Sheriff Paul let loose a bark of a laugh, "No sir. Matter of fact I don't have much use for you here at all so you can go ahead and perform your vanishing act now."

"You misunderstand me. I'm not asking."

"Are you trying to intimidate me?"

"Let me make this simple, Jim. One phone call and this station, this city, town, whatever you call it will be shut down. You and your men will be my men and I'll have you guarding your local livestock beauty contest until my business is done here. Don't make me make that call."

Sheriff Paul leaned forward in his chair, "You can go straight to hell, bub, and shove your cell phone up your ass on the way down. Now get the fuck out of my office."

Outside, Jack stood next to his car. He fished his phone from his pocket and flipped it open. The phone chirper and a robot voice requested his I.D.

"Carter, Guardian Seven Two Nine."

The phone chirped again and connected. "Jack?" A young man answered.

"I need a DHS auth faxed to this shithead Sheriff."

"DHS Auth?"

"Spencer, you need to get on this fast."

"Okay, okay." Spencer was sitting in a dim office surrounded by computer monitors. He rolled from one monitor to another typing commands, "Requesting?"

"Witness interaction."

"Witness… they have a witness?"

"Spencer."

"It's done." Spencer said as he tapped the enter key.

Jack closed his phone and opened the door to his car. He was about to climb in when he heard a voice shouting at him.

"Sir!"

Jack smirked and closed the car door. He turned and walked towards the deputy.

"Sheriff wants to see you."

"I figured he might."

Jack followed him into the station. The sheriff was standing next to his office with his arms crossed. Jack could see a crumpled sheet of paper in his hand.

"Department of Homeland Security?"

Jack shrugged.

The girl had pulled her legs up to her chest and had her arms wrapped around them. She rested her forehead on her knees. She looked up when Jack entered. Her eyes were still wet.

"Are my parents here?" she asked.

Jack pulled out a chair and sat down across from her, "Not yet. They should be soon though."

"There's blood on my shoes."

"I'm sorry." Jack said, "It must have been a terrible sight."

She shrugs, "I just wanna go home."

"I'm sure. That's what I would want. Your parents will be here soon. Can you tell me your name?"

"Destiny."

Jack leaned forward and flipped off the microphone on the table. "Let's have us a private chat, Destiny. It's just you and me. No fat sheriff listening in."

"Okay."

"What is your name?"

"I already told you. It's Destiny."

"What is your real name?"

"I don't understand."

Jack leaned forward again, "Pacha Nor Daya Nara."

Destiny flinched as if she had been slapped. Her eyes narrowed.

"I've been following you for weeks." Jack said, "I thought you would be a famous pop star by now. Give me your real name."

"I'll cut my own tits off before I tell you my name."

"Does that mean you are female? That will narrow the list down considerably. Traya? Sia? Allaga?"

"Don't presume to know us all. We are legion and we are infinity." Her face shifted slightly as she said this and for a moment Jack thought she was going to attack but she simply leaned back and flipped her hair over her shoulder.

"You're scaring me, mister." Back to the kid bit, "Do you know what scared feels like?" Or not.

Jack heard a crash from outside the interview room.

"You can call off your tricks." Jack said.

"It's not my trick. It's my pet."

Jack stood and rushed to the door. He yanked it open and saw carnage before him.

A large dog-like beast was ripping Sheriff Paul's insides out. It chewed the bloodied tubes for a moment before tossing them aside and going in for more. Jack looked away but everywhere his eyes moved was more gore. He noticed a pile of heads in the center of the room. As he glanced away he saw the Sheriff's head join the stack.

The dog-beast clacked across the floor. It had no fur and its flesh was deep red. It seemed moist as if every step excreted some kind of bile over its entire body. The creature turned its head towards Jack and seemed to sniff the air. It had no eyes, just jagged spikes in their place.

Jack quickly closed the door and turned to Destiny. He pulled a gun from inside his jacket.

"I order you back from whence you came. By the or…"

"You don't have my name, Carter."

Jack cocked his gun.

"I don't need your name to kill you." He pulled the trigger. The bullet ripped into her head and spread the remains against the wall behind her.

"Back to the dark place, Demon."

Jack stepped around the table and put three more rounds into the rapidly deteriorating body. Thick green smoke rose from the body. He tilted his head and listened. He heard nothing from the other room. He opened the door, saw that the beast was gone and left the station.

Manny

Spring, 1969

SUNLIGHT STREAMED DOWN THROUGH THE TREES, SENDING pillars of light to the forest floor. The sounds of birds and rustling leaves filled the air around the small wooden cabin. A short ways away from the cabin a young boy sat at a picnic table. He was hunched over something, his hands busily working at his task. Every few seconds a clicking sound rang out as he worked.

Inside the cabin, the boy's mother stood at the stove frying bologna and eggs. Her husband Martin shuffled out of the bedroom dressed up in his work clothes.

"Mmm-hmm that smells mighty good darlin'. You make sure and fix me up a good size plate of that."

"You'll get your breakfast as soon as you see what your boy

is doin' down there by the lake. He's been sittin' at that table for nearly an hour."

"Esther, let the boy go about his business. He's growin' up, he deserves his privacy." said Martin, as he sat at the table.

"I'm worried Martin. I can't help bein' a mother." Esther turned down the flames on the stove, "Now go on and check, move now."

"Aw hell." Martin stood up and made his way out of the house. He looked down the path towards the lake and the picnic table.

"Manny! Boy get up here breakfast is ready!"

Manny paid no attention to his father's call. He kept his eyes locked on what he was doing. His father stomped his way down the path.

"Boy you lost your hearing? I said breakfast is ready."

Manny ignored him. Martin reached forward and tapped his son's shoulder. Manny leapt up and spun to face his father. He held a blood-covered knife in his hand. Martin flinched when he saw the look on his son's face.

"Sweet Jesus boy. What are you doing with that knife?" He looked past Manny and saw a frog cut to pieces on the table, "Have you gone half out of your damn mind?"

Manny looked at his father. His face was void of any emotion. Martin grabbed the knife from him.

"You get on up to the house. You're in a right load of trouble. I'm gonna whip the black right off you boy." Martin shoved Manny towards the house. He looked at the cut up frog and shook his head then followed his son to the house.

The smell of frying bologna filled the cabin. Martin told Manny to go on into the back yard then went into the kitchen.

"Esther love you was right to be worried."

Esther picked up the frying pan and walked to the kitchen table.

"What was he doin?" She asked as she scooped the slices of bologna onto a plate in the center of the table.

"He was cuttin' up a bullfrog. Just stabbing it, over and over."

Esther looked up at Martin, a horrified look on her face.

"When I called him he didn't even hear me. It was like he was in some kinda trance. He didn't know I was even there till I touched him. Then he turned like he was gonna knife me!" Martin pulled off his hat and scratched his head, "I hate to do it, but I'm gonna have to take a belt to him."

Esther sat down in a chair; she held her hand against her chest.

"I best make it quick." Martin walked out of the kitchen to the hall that led to his room. He walked into the bedroom and to the closet. He pulled open the closet door and as he was reaching for his belt he heard his wife scream in terror. He slammed the closet door shut and turned to see Manny standing they're holding half of the frog carcass in his hand.

"Son of a bitch boy!" Martin grabbed Manny's arm and dragged him out of the house. He pushed him towards the chopping block. "Now you lean down there and take your punishment. You can't be killin' like that. I have to teach you a lesson. It's only cause I love you."

Manny placed his hands on the chopping block. His eyes locked on the hatchet that was imbedded in the wood. He flinched as he felt the belt strike his back the first time. Tears welled up in his eyes as his father continued to strike him with the belt. Manny's eyes remained on the hatchet. His vision became blurred as the pain radiated through him. He felt the rage begin to build within him. He saw his hand move and grip the hatchet handle. He felt himself spin and yank the hatchet from the chopping block. He felt the cool air rush past him as he spun and buried the hatchet in his father's chest. He watched the blood shoot upwards as he raised the hatchet and slammed it into his father again and again.

Esther stood up from her chair. She wiped her hands on a towel and walked to the kitchen sink. She looked out the window and saw Martin begin to whip Manny. She closed her eyes and lowered her head. When she heard the whipping sounds stop she let herself look out the window again. Her shrill scream filled the forest around her. Her eyes locked with Manny's. His eyes were wild. He held a bloody hatchet in his hand. He was covered in gore.

"Sweet god in heaven." Esther whispered. She ran out of the kitchen into the hallway. She ran into her bedroom and grabbed the phone. She hadn't even dialed a number when the window above the bed shattered and her husband's head bounced off the wall then rolled to a stop in front of her. She screamed loudly and ran out of the bedroom to the front door. She yanked the door open. Her eyes widened and she screamed. Manny stood before her, drenched in his father's blood. He looked up at her, his face contorted in rage. He raised the hatchet into the air and slammed it into her chest.

The soft singing of the birds stopped. The only sound filling the forest is that of Manny's hatchet striking into his mother's dying body.

***

Today...

"This concludes your afternoon announcements, please keep in mind that spring break is still two days away so any of you not here tomorrow will be marked absent. Have a nice day."

The bell rang loudly and students flooded into the hallways. The roar of their chatter bounced off Garrett Saranno's ears. He sat alone on a bench outside the office. He vaguely heard his friends walk up to him. His girlfriend Colleen sat next to him and put her arm around his shoulder.

"Garrett, are you okay?"

Garrett looked over at Colleen then up at his other friends that stood around him. He lowered his head and sighed.

"I… my Uncle Charlie died today."

"Oh dude… Uncle Charlie? That sucks man. He was a cool guy."

"I know Dave. I have to go to the funeral tomorrow and the reading of his will on Saturday. So I can't go with you guys on your trip."

Colleen took Garrett's hand in hers. She squeezed it tightly.

"Garrett, we all knew your uncle. He was a friend to all of us. I think we should all go with you to the funeral."

"Are you sure?"

"Yeah dude." Dave patted his friend's shoulder.

"Hey why is everyone so sad looking?"

Garrett looked up and saw Dave's girlfriend Lauren walking up to them.

"Hi Lauren." Colleen pushed her blonde hair back and smiled slightly.

Dave grabbed Lauren and hugged her.

"Uncle Charlie died today." Dave said.

"Garrett's Uncle?"

"Yeah."

"Oh Garrett I'm sorry. Are you okay?"

"Yeah, I'm fine." Garrett rubbed his face and looked towards the door, "I'm going to head home. I guess I'll see you all tomorrow?"

Colleen squeezed his hand.

"What time should we come?"

Garrett stood up and put his backpack over his shoulders.

"About nine I guess. See ya." Garrett walked down the hall and went outside. He pulled his car keys from his pocket and got into his car.

Colleen looked over at her friends. She smiled apologetically at them, "You guys don't have to go to the funeral. I'll stay and go with Garrett, you guys go ahead and go to Laguna."

"No way, we're going." said Dave. He took Lauren's hand in his, "Right baby?"

"Yeah, of course." She said, "Someone better tell André and Kendra."

"I'll call Kendra when I get home." Colleen said as she stood up "Can you call André, Dave?"

"Will do."

"See ya Colleen."

Colleen waved as she headed out of the school. Dave and Lauren turned and walked the opposite direction.

The air on Friday morning was moist with predawn rain. The birds sang happily as the long trail of cars made its way along the cemetery road.

Garrett sat in the back of a black limousine staring out the darkened window. He did his best to stay strong for his mother and himself. They had been through a lot the past couple of years. First Garrett's father died in a car crash, now Uncle Charlie's heart attack.

Garrett turned in his seat and looked out the back window. He saw his friends following closely in Colleen's jeep. He smiled to himself. He knew they were distraught over his uncle's death as well. Uncle Charlie had been a friend to them all. He coached Garret and the other guys in basketball every Saturday for the past two years. Garrett returned his gaze out through the side window as the limousine began to slow. He reached over and took his mother's hand and smiled at her.

"It'll be okay." He said to her. She smiled at him and nodded slowly.

The service was short. Garrett had his arm around his mother comforting her as her body shook with sobs. Colleen held his other hand tightly and laid her head on his shoulder.

"So we now commit this body to the earth. Ashes to ashes dust to dust. Amen." The priest closed his bible and nodded to the crowd. He stepped back as the coffin began to lower into the hole.

Garrett rubbed his mother's back as she continued to sob. He looked at Colleen and smiled his thanks. She smiled back and walked with Dave and Lauren to the jeep.

"Come on Mom, let's get going."

"No, I… I need to stay here."

"Mom, please." Garrett tugged her slightly and they slowly walked to the limousine. Garrett helped her into the car. He pushed the door shut and walked over to Colleen's jeep.

"You okay?" she asked.

"Yeah I'm good. André and Kendra know about Laguna?"

"Yeah. I called André. He wasn't too happy." Dave leaned against the jeep; "He can be an asshole sometimes."

"Well fuck him. I can't help what happened." Garrett ran his hand through his hair; "Maybe we can go somewhere after the reading of Uncle Charlie's will."

"If you feel up to it." Lauren said as she leaned against Dave.

The limousine driver honked the horn. Garrett turned and waved to him.

"I gotta go guys. I'll call you tomorrow afternoon okay?"

"Okay dude." Dave took Lauren's hand and they got into the car.

"Thanks for coming." Garrett said as he wrapped his arms around Colleen. She kissed him softly.

"He was a good man Garrett."

"Yeah. I better go." Garrett kissed her again and walked to the limousine.

Colleen waved to him and got into the driver's side of her jeep.

The limousine driver started the car and drove out of the cemetery.

Garrett held his mother's hand on the way back to their house. She didn't stop crying until late that night when she finally fell asleep.

***

Garrett stood outside his Uncle's small house and took a deep breath. He glanced at his watch. There was an hour before the reading of the will. Garrett walked up the cracked sidewalk to the front door and fished the spare set of keys from his pocket. He unlocked the door and pushed it open. It creaked loudly as it swung inward.

Garrett walked down the short hall calling for his uncle's cat. His mother had ordered him to come here and find him.

"Here Kitty…" Garrett walked into the living room. The shades were drawn, shrouding the room in darkness, "Peejoe, here kitty kitty."

Something fell behind Garrett. He spun around and squinted in the dark. He stepped forward and squinted his eyes to try to see better. "Where are you Peejoe, you stupid ass cat."

Garrett leaped back in terror when the cat leapt at him from the mantle. The cat hissed loudly at him.

"Jesus!" Garret bent over and scooped up the cat, "Crazy bastard."

***

The lawyer's office was hot and dusty. Garrett and his mother sat before the lawyer's desk. Garrett's mother wiped tears from her eyes with her handkerchief.

"I'm sorry for the temperature in here. The air conditioning has broken again. I'll try to make this as brief as possible. Seeing as you two are Charlie's only living relatives he has left everything to you. There are a few things he left to each one of you separately. To you Garrett your uncle has given you his summer cottage in Stranger Lake. And for you Miss Saranno he has given you his house here in town. The rest can be divided up between you. That includes his assets."

"Is that all?" Garrett asked.

"Yes, that's everything. My secretary will provide you with a copy of his will." The lawyer reached into his desk drawer and pulled out a set of keys. He tossed the key to Garrett.

"These are the keys to the cabin. My secretary has the directions."

"Thank you, sir." Garrett stood up and took his mother's hand. He led her out of the office.

"I'll meet you in the car Mom." His mother nodded and walked out the door. Garrett turned to the secretary, "You have some things for me?"

"Yes." The secretary pulled out a large manila envelope and handed it to Garrett; "I'm very sorry for your loss."

"Thanks." Garrett took the envelope and walked out. He sat in the driver's seat of his mother's car and started it.

"I'll take you home Mom, then I have to go see Colleen. Are you gonna be okay?"

"Yes Garrett. Thanks. You go see your friends."

"I shouldn't be too long."

They drove the rest of the way in silence. Garrett's mother stared out the window and cried softly. Garrett sighed heavily as he pulled the car into the driveway. He walked his mom to the door and let her inside.

"I already fed Peejoe. I'll come back in a while."

"Okay Garrett."

Garrett kissed her goodbye and went back to the car.

"So is this spring break a complete waste? Garrett's Uncle drops dead and we get screwed out of a week at Laguna Beach."

"Kendra shut up." said Colleen, "Garrett didn't plan this to happen. He was looking forward to Laguna as much as you were."

"Well André is pissed."

"I don't care what André is."

Colleen lay back on her bed. She looked over at Kendra who was sitting at her desk typing on the computer.

"Is that the only reason you came here?" Colleen asked.

"Mainly."

"You are such a b…" Colleen stopped talking when she heard something at her window, "What the hell was that?" she whispered.

Kendra walked towards the window.

"Kendra!" Colleen hissed at her. Kendra waved her arm at Colleen and stepped in front of the window.

"It's nearly five o'clock Colleen, who's gonna try to break in this early?" Kendra looked back at the window and leapt back when someone pounded loudly on it."

"Mother Fucker!" shouted Kendra, "You stupid shit!" She leaned forward and yanked the window open.

André pulled himself inside and grinned wildly, "Hey baby."

"Don't hey baby me. You scared the hell out of us."

"Calm down no one's gonna hurt you while I'm here."

"Oh sure. Big bad football boy's gonna protect us." Colleen said sarcastically.

"You know it." Said André, "oh, your boy is downstairs on the porch."

"Garrett?"

"Who else?"

Colleen jumped up and ran downstairs. She pulled the front door open and saw Garrett standing there. She smiled brightly and hugged him tightly.

"How'd it go?"

"It went fine. I got some good news."

"What?"

"We get to go on a trip after all. Uncle Charlie left me a cottage in his will."

"A cottage? Where at?"

"Some place called Stranger Lake."

"I've never heard of it." Colleen took Garrett's hand and led him to her room, "Hey guys, guess what."

"You're pregnant." said André seriously.

"No you ass. Garrett's taking us to his new cottage."

"Cottage?" André stood up causing Kendra to fall to the floor, "What the fuck would we want to go to a cottage for?"

"My Uncle left it to me in his will. I want to go check it out. It'll be fun. It's on a lake."

"Whoop dee fuckin doo." mumbled André.

"I figured we could leave tomorrow morning. We'd probably get there in a few hours. It's just a little ways upstate I think."

"Great. We get to visit the hicks of Washington. If I see one dude in a white robe I'm kicking your ass." André made a fist, "I ain't kidding either."

***

Dave slammed the rear hatch closed and walked around to the driver's side. He handed Garrett the keys to his dad's Navigator.

"You wreck this and my dad will kick both our asses."

Garrett smirked and got in the truck. Colleen got in the passenger side. The others got in the back.

"Here we go." said Garrett as he started the car and pulled away from the curb.

They rode in silence for a while, each engrossed in their thoughts. Garrett flipped his way through the radio stations until he found a song he liked. André and Kendra were fast asleep in the back.

"I'm glad we decided to do this Garrett," said Colleen, "who knows what's gonna happen after graduation. This could be the last thing we all do together, y'know?"

Garrett smiled at her and grabbed her hand.

"Don't get too happy. Let me find the place first."

"You better get us there fast, I gotta piss." André said as he stretched his arms.

"We're almost there."

"I hope so."

"Where'd I put the map?" asked Garrett, he turned in his seat and looked at the back seat.

"Why do you need the map? You said we're almost there." said André.

Garrett reached back for the map.

"Oh God, Garrett, look out!"

Garrett looked back at the road. He saw the dog walking across the street.

\

"Oh shit!" He shouted as he jerked the wheel. The car lurched slightly and Garrett squealed to a stop, "Oh fuck, did I hit it? Did I hit it?"

Garrett jumped out of the car; "You guys stay here." He walked back to where the dog lay in the road. He crouched down near the dog and sighed.

"This is just great. Really great." Garrett walked back to the truck and yanked open the door; "I hit it. Is there a blanket here I can wrap it up in?"

"Yeah here I'll help you." Dave got out and opened the back of the truck. He dug out a blanket and followed Garrett back to where the dog was.

"What the hell?" Garrett muttered.

"Dude, where's the dog?"

"I don't know. I thought it was dead."

"Well I guess you thought wrong." Dave walked back to the truck, "Come on man it's almost dark."

Garrett looked around and sighed then went back to the truck.

"What the hell happened out there?" André asked.

"I don't know it was fucking laying there, then it wasn't."

"Can we go now please? I'm cramping." whined Kendra.

"Oh fuck no. Garrett find this bitch a store get her some chocolate or some shit." said André.

Garrett turned the radio up and started to drive a little faster.

"Hey Dave," whispered Lauren.

"Yeah?"

"We're going to Stranger Lake right?"

"Yeah, why?"

"Well, my Dad used to tell us stories about that place, I mean really freaky stories, he said once that…"

Lauren was cut off when Garrett turned off the radio, "Hey

guys I'm gonna turn into this store and pick up some stuff for tonight, Dave come help me will ya?"

"Yo get some forties."

Dave and Garrett walked into the store. Dave walked back to the coolers while Garrett went up to the counter.

"Hello?" Garrett called out. He noticed a small bell on the counter and began tapping it. Garrett gasped loudly when someone grabbed his shoulder.

"I can hear ya fine boy. I'd thank ya kindly to stop banging on that bell."

"Oh, sorry." Garrett pulled his hand away from the bell.

"That's better," the old black man shuffled his way back behind the counter, "Now what can I help ya with?"

"I uh, my friends and I are going to my uncle's cabin up on Stranger Lake. Can you tell me how to get there?"

"Boy I can sure tell you something. You best get back in your car and turn right around and go back to whatever city you came from." The old man hacked loudly. "There ain't nothing up there for a bunch a kids to do."

"We just wanted to get away for spring break. My uncle just died and left me his cabin so we decided to come up here and check it out."

The old man scratched his head and coughed loudly then spoke again in his ragged voice.

"I'm sorry about your uncle, but you don't want to go up to that lake. Sure as sun shines that's a bad place. Things happened up there. Bad things."

Garrett jumped slightly when the bell over the door rang loudly.

"Hey Garrett, the girls want some Cheetos and Diet Coke." said André.

Garrett glanced at the old man then followed André to the back of the store.

"Dave let's get the beer and go."

"Dude what's wrong?"

"That guy's freaking me out. He's talking crazy about bad things going on at the lake."

André looked down the aisle at the old man who was staring at them, "That geezer better not start talking no Friday the 13th Jason slaughter house shit to me. I'll kick his a-."

"Shut up dude just grab the food and let's get the hell out of here." interrupted Garrett.

The three of them got what they came for and walked up to the counter. The old man added up the price.

"67.50." he said through a coughing fit.

"Watch that shit man. Don't be hacking your shit on my Doritos man." said André.

Garrett pulled out his wallet and handed seventy dollars to the man. André and Dave grabbed the stuff and walked out of the store. Garrett took his change and grabbed the last bag and followed them. He walked towards the car and stumbled, a bag of Cheetos fell to the ground.

"Shit." said Garrett as he crouched over to grab the bag.

"Don't go up there." the old man said as he grabbed Garrett's arm.

"Fuck!" shouted Garrett as he leapt back.

"He's all grown up now. He don't take kindly to visitors."

Garrett yanked his arm away and walked to the truck. André stood next to the truck and pointed at the old man, "You keep that freaky deeky Jason shit to yourself old man."

The old man just shook his head and watched as they got in the car and drove off.

Garrett looked out the back window of their truck as they sped away from the store. He watched the old man turn and walk back inside.

"What was that guy saying to you?" Colleen asked.

Garrett turned back in his seat and looked over at her, "Nothing. Just some crazy old people babbling."

"Garrett, who was he talking about? I heard him say something about some guy not liking visitors." Colleen looked at Garrett then back at the road.

"I don't know who he was talking about. Just drive okay? We're almost there."

Colleen sighed and kept her attention on the road, however she couldn't ignore the sense of dread in her gut.

A short time later they pulled up in front of a decent sized log cabin.

"Whoa dude this place is great!" yelled Dave from the back.

"Yeah." Garrett said solemnly.

Colleen parked the car and everyone got out. Garrett walked around the front of the car and fished the key to the front door out of his pocket. He slowly walked up the dirt path to the porch. He shakily moved to insert the key when a loud horn blasted nearby.

"Hey, you kids supposed to be here?"

They all turned and saw a large green pickup idling behind them.

"This is private property, ya know." The two men in the truck were looking angrily at André and Kendra.

"You better turn your big ugly head away from me you inbred cross-eyed lard ass." André mumbled under his breath, "I'll be kicking some fat ass today."

"This is my uncle's cabin mister." Garrett said as he walked back down to the truck, "We're supposed to be here."

"Well all right then. We're gonna be down the way a bit out on the lake fishing. Lyle here tends to pass out drunk in the boat so don't be worried if we don't come back by."

"Oh I'm sure we'd be worried sick." said Kendra sarcastically.

The fisherman sped off down the dirt road leaving thick dust trail behind them

"Assholes." shouted Kendra.

Garrett walked back up to the door of the cabin and unlocked it. He pushed the door open and went inside. He looked around the large den and kitchen. There were white sheets over all the furniture.

"There hasn't been anyone here for a while." mumbled Garrett.

"How can ya tell?" asked Dave sarcastically.

Garrett moved out of the way as is friends started to bring in their stuff.

"Does the fridge work?" asked André.

"Yeah I can hear it going. I'm surprised the electricity is still on." said Garrett as he walked out to get his things. He walked down to the truck and saw Lauren standing with her arms crossed looking out into the woods.

"Hey Lauren are you okay?"

Lauren jumped slightly and turned to Garrett.

"I'm fine. Just a little y'know. I'm fine." She reached down and grabbed her bags than walked to the house. Garrett pulled his things out of the back and slammed the rear hatch closed. He looked out into the woods when he heard a twig snap. He didn't see anything so he picked his bags up from the ground and carried them into the cabin. He shut and locked the door behind him.

***

"Wait just a damn minute Lyle. I said no fancy stuff." Darryl looked at the bottle of brandy and shook his head. "Can't you ever bring just regular beer? Why is it always rich people shit? Hell I can't drink it ain't no way. I'll be shitting all night. You know that. Remember last time?" Darryl reached into his bag and pulled out a large bottle of tequila, "Now this is the stuff," he said as he opened it and took a drink.

Darryl and Lyle put their gear into the small rowboat they kept hidden on the riverbank and shoved it into the water. They hopped inside it and rowed out to the center of the lake. They quickly dropped the lines into the water and started drinking. They had a hell of a day and planned on forgetting it real quick.

Lyle nursed his bottle of brandy and leaned back, "When's the last time we caught something?"

"Well, I got that big one a few days back. What was he, a six pounder?"

"That was ten years ago you stupid son of a bitch. 'Sides it was only four pounds."

"Four my ass. Ten pounds at least."

"You just said six!"

"I was mistaken." Darryl took another swig from his tequila. "Least I've caught something."

Lyle scoffed and took a drink of his brandy. He looked towards the shore and saw something move along the shore.

"Hey Darryl, there's somethin' over there."

"Ah hell Lyle. You say that every time we come out here." Darryl turned around and looked at the shore. Nothing seemed to be unusual. "There ain't nothing over there. You need to quit drinking. First step to getting help is admitting you have a problem."

The two fishermen looked at each other and began to laugh hysterically.

From the woods came a loud crashing sound. Both men stopped laughing and looked towards shore.

"Now you can't tell me that was nothin', Darryl. That sure as day was somethin'."

"Just a bear."

Lyle reeled in his hook and set the rod down on the bottom of the boat and picked up the oars.

"Now what in Sam hell are you doing?"

"Goin' bear huntinhuntin'."

Lyle rowed the small boat up to the shore. He jumped out and pulled the boat up onto the ground. "Come on Darryl."

"Now Lyle, let's go back and get the guns. We don't know what's out here."

"Aw hell. Don't be yella." Lyle walked up ahead along a worn trail into the thick forest. Darryl looked back at the boat and then back towards the trail. He couldn't see Lyle at all.

"Lyle? Lyle!" He stepped forward towards the trees, "You crazy old codger come back here!"

Darryl squinted to see into the dark trees. He heard a twig snap nearby.

"That you Lyle?"

Darryl stepped towards the tree line. Something moved quickly in front of him. Darryl had just enough time to see the hulking dark shape leap at him before his head fell from his shoulders. His lifeless body fell to the dirt.

The dark figure crouched down and picked up Darryl's head. He walked off into the woods with a severed head in one hand and a bloody sickle in the other.

***

The living room was bathed in orange light as a fire blazed in the fireplace. Garrett sat on the floor in front of Colleen who was lying on the couch. Dave and Lauren were making out in the corner. André and Kenya were upstairs doing a bit more, their friends suspected.

"I'm glad we came up here." Colleen whispered into Garrett's ear.

"I am too." Garrett smiled up at her.

Dave and Lauren stood up and walked to the door.

"We're gonna go for a walk by the lake." Lauren said, "Don't wait up."

Dave grinned and followed her out the door.

Garrett stood up and walked to the fireplace. He picked up the poker and shoved the logs around some.

"What's wrong Garrett?"

"Nothing Col, I was just thinking about that old man at the store."

"Why? What did he say to you?"

Garrett thought about the man's warning.

"Garrett?"

Garrett turned and looked at Colleen. He walked over and sat on the couch with her, "Don't worry about it. He was halfway to senile anyway." He wrapped his arms around her and kissed her.

"Well that was nice." she giggled.

***

"Dave? Let's go back. It's cold."

"Come on Lauren it's not that cold. Let's just go to the docks and sit for a while okay?"

"Dave, it's too cold."

"Fine here." Dave pulled off his jacket and handed it to her.

"Wear this." Lauren took the jacket and put it on.

"Thank you."

Dave walked slightly ahead of Lauren. He was walking too fast for her to keep up.

"Slow down, will you?" Lauren said.

"Come on run if ya have to." Dave called back.

"Dammit Dave, slow down or I'm going back!" Lauren shouted after Dave. He disappeared around a bend into the woods, "Dave?"

Lauren walked around the bend and looked down the path. Dave was nowhere in sight.

"Oh god. Dave?!" She yelled, "This isn't funny! Come out now!"

Lauren heard something in the woods. She looked into the dark trees.

"Dave you asshole, come out!"

Lauren nearly leapt out of her skin when she felt something grab her shoulder. She spun around and screamed.

"Jesus Lauren! Calm down." Dave said.

"You asshole!"

"What? I was taking a piss!"

"That's all your gonna be using that for." Lauren pushed her way past Dave and walked towards the house.

"Lauren come on!"

She just flipped her middle finger at him.

"Fine, I'll be at the dock." Dave turned and walked down the path.

***

Garrett sat up and pulled his shirt off. He leaned forward and kissed Colleen on the neck. He unbuttoned her shirt slowly and kissed her each time where new flesh was exposed. She sat up and undid her bra.

Garrett smiled and kissed her. He took her in his hands and pressed himself against her.

The front door burst open causing Garrett and Colleen to separate quickly. Colleen pulled her shirt over herself as Lauren slammed the door shut.

"Fucking asshole!" she screamed then looked at Garrett and Colleen, "Oh sorry, I didn't mean…"

"It's okay." Garrett pulled his shirt back on.

"What happened?" Colleen asked as she buttoned her shirt.

"Dave scared me. Stupid prick. He'll be spanking it tonight." Lauren walked up the stairs and slammed the door to her room shut.

Garrett and Colleen just looked at each other.

***

Dave sat on the edge of the deck and stared up at the sky. The lake stretched out before him. The water was a deep black, almost like oil, and smooth as silk. Crickets and owls chirped and hooted through the woods. Dave heard a thudding sound behind him.

"I knew you couldn't stay away." Dave said still staring ahead of him.

The footsteps stopped.

"Come sit down Lauren, it's beautiful out here."

Something dropped on the dock and rolled towards Dave. It bumped into his side. Dave looked down at it and screamed. He jumped up and turned towards the person behind him. He had no time to scream again. The man before him raised his arm up and buried his sickle in Dave's face.

Dave gurgled and fell to the dock. The man crouched over and grabbed the head he rolled at Dave. Then he grabbed Dave's collar and dragged him off into the woods.

***

"Did you hear something?"

André pulled his pants up and looked over at Kendra.

"Nope."

"I thought I heard a scream."

"Girl you just heard that weed I gave you. It's speaking to you. Let it talk."

"No André, I'm serious. Someone screamed outside."

André walked to the window, he pulled back the curtain and looked outside.

"There ain't nothing out there Kendra. Just leaves and trees and woods and shit."

"I heard something I'm telling you." Kendra got up out of bed and pulled her shirt on.

"André! Kendra! I'm going back to the store you want anything?" Garrett screamed from the bottom of the stairs.

André grabbed his shirt and pulled it over his head.

"Hold on man, I'll come with you." André said to Garrett, "You want anything from the store baby?"

"Surprise me." Kendra said as she looked out the window.

"I'll surprise you when I get back." André said as he kissed her.

"You better have a vibrator then." she cracked.

"What? Bitch you better…"

"André! Let's go!" Garrett yelled.

"Coming!" yelled André, then huskily to Kendra, "you better be ready for me when I get back."

Kendra snickered as he left the room.

***

Garrett turned the truck onto the main road and sped up. André sat in the seat next to him drumming his fingers on the dashboard.

"Why are we going back here anyway?" He asked.

Garrett glanced over at him, then back at the road.

"Don't be all mysterious and shit G."

"I want to know more about what that old guy was talking about."

"Aww shit Garrett. Man, if you would have told me that earlier I woulda stayed in bed."

"You can stay in the car then."

"Hell no I ain't staying in the car. I just smoked a fatty with Kendra man. I gots to eat."

Garrett just shook his head as he pulled into the store's parking lot. The entire place looked dark.

"Well, nobody home. Let's go back."

Garrett ignored him and pressed his fingers down on the horn. The store remained dark.

"I guess he's not here." Garrett said.

André and Garrett both jumped when something pounded on the driver's window.

"FUCK!" André screamed.

Garrett rolled the window down.

"I figured you'd come back." said the old man, "Come inside then."

***

"Has Dave come back yet?"

Colleen turned away from the fireplace and looked at Lauren.

"No. I haven't seen him. Maybe he went with André and Garrett."

94

"He was down at the docks. He wouldn't have known they were going."

"Well if he was coming back when they left he would have seen them."

"Yeah," Lauren sat down on the couch, "I guess you're right."

Colleen sat down next to her.

"We could go down to the docks and look if you want."

"Okay." Lauren got up and walked to the door, Colleen grabbed her coat and followed her outside, "It's just down this path I think."

***

"I wanna know about what you told me earlier." Garrett sat down at the old man's table.

"Well son, I can tell you all you want to know."

"Hey old guy, can I go get some chips and something to eat?" André said from the doorway.

"Yes. The keys are right there. Don't touch that register or I'll whoop your black ass. I may be old but I can whoop you a good one."

André just stood there a second. He then grabbed the keys and walked outside. The old man pulled a cigar from his pocket and lit it up.

"Earlier today you mentioned someone. You said he was all grown up. Who were you talking about?"

"Right to the point I see. Not one for pleasant conversation are you boy?" The old man puffed on his cigar, "I was talking about a boy I knew long ago. Round about 1969 I guess it was. His name was Manny. Scrawny little black boy about twelve I think. Him and his parents lived back there on the far side of the lake."

"Sir I don't see what this has to do with us. We just came here to see my uncle's cabin for the week."

"Let me finish," he puffed on his cigar again, "One day in the spring Manny's father found him taking a knife to a frog. Just a stabbing it and stabbing it." The old man made stabbing motions with his hands as he spoke, "His father was furious. He took Manny out back and just went to whooping him. He took a belt to him, he did. Well he had Manny bent over a tree stump that he used to chop wood for the fireplace. I guess Manny just lost that little bit of humanity he had left. He took that hatchet his father had stuck there and he just started swinging. He hacked his father pretty good. Used his head to scare his mother half to death. He met her at the front door as she was running. He hacked her good as well. She didn't die from that though. Looked to be she died of fright when she opened the door. Her heart just burst from fear. Anyway make a long story short that boy disappeared."

"Disappeared? For thirty years? How does someone disappear for thirty years? How does he eat?"

"I don't know nothin' about that."

"How do you know so much about this?"

"Well that's should be pretty clear I think. I was a deputy for the sheriff when it happened."

"Why didn't you catch him?

"Like I said. He disappeared. He knew these woods pretty well I'd say. As the years went on the town died. There was no need for a police force. Everyone left. I stayed and opened this store."

"This is crazy." Garrett stood up. The old man slammed his hand on the table.

"I ain't finished yet!"

Garrett sat back down.

"Now you listen close. Every few years or so some people get wind of that story and they come lookin' for something they don't want to find. Last time was about ten years ago. I figured it was over with. I wouldn't have to ward off anyone else. That last group that came through never went home. I never saw them again after they left here. Now I'm telling you. Go back and get your girls and your other pal and get yourself home. Manny is still around here. And he still has a taste for the killing."

***

"Colleen, he's not here."
The two girls stood at the beginning of the dock.
"Well he must have went with Garrett."
Lauren looked towards the end of the dock.
"What is that?"
"What?"
"There's something on the dock. What is it?"

***

"Hello? Where is everybody?" Kendra stood at the bottom of the stairs, she was wearing a long T-shirt that barely covered her. She was naked beneath it. "Colleen?" She turned to go into the kitchen when she heard a creaking on the porch. Kendra walked to the front door and pulled it open, "Lauren?" She stepped outside and looked around.

"Where the hell is everybody?" Kendra stepped off the porch and looked down the path towards the lake. She placed her hands on her hips. She listened closely to the sounds of the forest around her. She heard something behind her and quickly turned around.

The man before her was huge. He towered above her. Kendra saw the sharp bloodstained sickle in his hand and opened her

97

mouth to scream. The man quickly swung the sickle and sliced her from groin to shoulder. Kendra's face froze, her scream caught in her throat. Her body split and fell to the ground on opposite sides of the walkway.

***

"What is it Colleen?"

Colleen knelt down and touched her fingers to the stain on the dock. She brought her fingers to her nose and smelled them.

"Oh my god." she whispered and began to shake.

***

"The girls are in the house alone!" Garrett shouted as he sped back towards the cabin.

"I don't know why you believe what this guy is saying! You don't even know him!"

"I'm telling the truth." The old man said calmly.

"You're saying some kid hacked his parents to death then disappeared into the woods for thirty years. What kid can live in the woods for thirty years! I tell you what G, the Viagra is having the wrong effect on this guy."

"Shut up André!" Garrett quickly turned onto the road to the cabin sending a spray of gravel into the air.

***

"Colleen? Oh my god. What is it?"

"It's b-blood."

Both girls jumped when they heard someone step onto the dock. Lauren was the first one to start screaming.

***

Garrett leaped out of his truck and ran up to the house. He burst inside and screamed for Colleen.

"Oh shit man."

Garrett looked outside and saw that André was sitting on the walkway.

"What are you doing?"

"I fucking slipped," André stood up and wiped his hand across the back of his pants, "Oh fuck, Garrett man I think it's blood man."

"We're too late." The old man was standing near the truck looking towards them when the screaming started, "He's already here."

***

"Shhhh! Shut up Goddamnit!" Lyle shouted at the girls.

"Stay away from us!" Lauren screamed.

Lyle held his hands out in front of him.

"It's okay!"

Lauren grabbed Colleen's arm.

"What do you want?" asked Colleen.

"My buddy is missing. We was looking in the woods for somethin'. I tripped and hit my head and I blacked out. Darryl was gone when I came to."

"Colleen!"

"Garrett!" Colleen ran down the dock and threw her arms around Garrett.

"Are you okay? I heard screaming."

"We found blood on the dock. I think it's Dave."

André looked past Colleen and Garrett.

"Where's Kendra?"

"She's in the house still." said Lauren

"Oh no. No, no way." André looked down at his blood-covered hand.

"André what is it?" asked Colleen.

"There was blood all over the sidewalk." Garrett said.

The old man finally made it to the docks. He walked to the group and tapped the fisherman on the shoulder.

"Lyle you go get in that truck and go on home."

"Carl you crazy old shit. I ain't goin' nowheres till I find Darryl."

"Go home Lyle. Darryl is dead. I been tellin' you for years not to come here now look what happened. Now get home!"

"Fuck that," Lyle pushed his way past Carl and began walking up the other path, "I ain't lettin' no crazy old nigger tell me what to do. You get your own black ass home. You ain't my daddy. Damn coons trying to tell the white man what to-." Lyle's sentence was cut off when his head fell from his shoulders.

Colleen and Lauren screamed.

"Holy fuck!" yelled André.

"Go Run!" Garrett shoved André and Lauren forward towards the path that went to the cabin. They all began to run. They could hear something thrashing through the trees next to them. Ahead of them the lights from the truck shined. André reached the truck first. He tried to open the back door. It was locked. The car was still running.

"Garrett! You fucking locked the keys in the car!"

Garrett yanked on the driver's side door. It wouldn't open.

"SHIT!" Garrett yelled, "Get in the house! Go fast!" The four of them ran inside the house. Garrett slammed the door and locked it.

"Garrett that old guy is still out there." Colleen said.

"Oh shit. I have to go help him."

"Fuck that! Let that old shit take care of himself!" André said.

"I have to help him. He helped us. I can't leave him alone out there."

"I'm going with you then." Colleen went to the fireplace and grabbed the poker. She walked back to Garrett and handed it to him.

Lauren was sitting on the couch sobbing.

"Stay with her André." Garrett said and walked outside.

André locked the door and rested his head against it.

***

"Carl!" Garrett yelled as he walked down the path, Colleen clung tightly to his arm. The woods around them were silent. They reached the end of the car headlights reach. The bright full moon did its best to light the path ahead of them.

"Garrett, let's go back."

"Look there he is!" Garrett pulled Colleen down the path.

Carl was lying on the ground. He looked up as they approached him.

"Why are you still here?"

"We came to get you." Colleen said.

"Help me up." Garrett and Colleen reached down and both grabbed one of Carl's arms. They helped him to his feet, "You should have just left me here. Where are the others?"

"They're at the house."

"Oh my god Garrett look out!" Colleen screamed as Manny leapt out of the woods. He collided with Garrett and they both fell to the ground. Garrett scrambled backwards and jumped to his feet. He swung the poker at Manny. It connected solidly with his head. Manny got to his feet, blood trickled down his forehead. Garrett swung the poker at him again. Manny caught his wrist. With his other hand, Manny yanked the poker from Garret's hand.

"GARRETT!" screamed Colleen

Manny shoved the poker up into Garrett's gut. He pushed the poker up until it pierced Garrett's throat. Garrett twitched and fell to the ground. Manny turned around and pulled his sickle from his belt.

"Run girl!" yelled Carl. Colleen and Carl began to run towards the house.

"ANDRE! OPEN THE FUCKING DOOR!" screamed Colleen.

André yanked open the front door and ran down the stairs. He saw Carl and Colleen running towards him. He could see Manny close behind them.

Colleen screamed in pain when Manny latched onto her hair.

"Colleen!" André ran towards her.

Manny raised his sickle into the air. André leaped into the air and crashed into Manny. They fell to the ground. Colleen scrambled to her feet. Manny shoved André away and got up quickly. André got to his feet and stood in front of Manny.

"Get in the house Colleen."

"André get away from him."

Carl grabbed a rock from near the porch.

"Come on you big bastard." André slugged Manny in the face, "You like that?" He punched Manny several times in the gut.

Manny backhanded André and sent him sprawling to the ground. Lauren grabbed Colleen's arm and tried to pull her towards the house.

"We can't help him!" Lauren shoved Colleen back towards the house.

"André!"

Manny raised his arm and launched his sickle through the air. It buried itself into Lauren's back. She fell against Colleen, blood sprayed from her mouth.

Colleen's eyes rolled back in her head and she fell to the ground unconscious.

Manny began walking towards her.

André got to his feet. He grabbed a large log from the ground.

"Chew on this mother fucker!" He spun around and slammed the log into Manny's face. André heard the truck speed towards them. He leaped out of the way just as the truck crashed into Manny sending him flying through the air. Carl slammed his foot on the gas. There was a sickening crunch as the truck rolled over Manny.

***

Carl moved the truck back in front of the house. He climbed out of the driver's seat and walked over to Colleen and André.

"She ain't wakin' up, man." André said shakily.

"Put her in the car. Buckle her into the seat." ordered Carl.

Carl walked past André into the house. André lifted Colleen into his arms and carried her to the truck. He put her into the passenger seat and pulled the seat belt around her. He looked up as Carl walked back out of the house carrying a blanket. He walked to the passenger side and handed it to André.

"Cover her up."

André nodded and put the blanket over Colleen. He shut the door and walked over to Carl.

"What now?" André asked.

"You get in that truck and you get on home."

"What about Garrett and Kendra?"

"I'll take care of it. I'll notify who needs to be notified."

The forest began to lighten as the sun rose into the sky. André walked to the truck and pulled the door open.

"This doesn't seem right, just leaving like this."

"Just go and get out of here."

André looked at Lauren's dead body lying in the grass then down the path.

"Go." commanded Carl.

André got into the truck and started it up. He reached out and pulled the door closed. He nodded at Carl and drove off.

Carl walked to the center of the road and watched as André drove down the road. He watched the truck disappear around a bend. He pulled his handkerchief out of his pocket and wiped his forehead. He sighed heavily and shook his head, returning the handkerchief to his pocket.

That would be the last thing Carl ever did. Two large hands grabbed his head and yanked it from his body.

Prelude

"And for the season it was winter, and they that know
the winters of that country know them to be sharp and
violent, and subject to cruel and fierce storms."
—William Bradford (1590 - 1657),
Of Plymouth Plantation

THERE WAS A SINGLE CANDLE BURNING. IT WAS A SINGLE ORANGE
glow among a hundred dead candles, a single orange glow against
the penetrating darkness inside the church.

It was once a grand cathedral filled with marble and gold. But
the tapestry faded, the marble cracked, the gold long moved away.

It became a shell, this church; it had not been used in years. Yet the candle still glowed.

The doors and windows were sealed, boarded over. Once a colorful, warm place of worship, it became grey and unwelcoming. Cobwebs stretched across the pews that were once red, but became grey with dust. The cavernous ceiling stretched high above, its peaks lost in darkness, save for one spot. A ragged hole revealed a patch of dim sky. A single snowflake fluttered through this hole. It lazily fell down, down, towards dust covered floor. A slight gust of wind sent it spiraling towards that beacon burning in the dark. With a hiss, the snowflake burned away.

The silence of the church was shattered by the loud shrill squeal of an age old nail being pulled from its home. A moment later, a loud creek filled the air as the door was slowly pushed open. A burst of wind forced itself into the church, causing the candle to flicker violently.

"Come on then. In here." A soft voice spoke. A girl of about nine years of age stepped through the door. She was bundled into a too large winter coat. Her head was hidden beneath a thick hat. Behind her, an older girl entered. Her blonde hair fell to her shoulders, her ears were covered by blue earmuffs, and a large backpack rested on her shoulders. She turned and leaned against the door, pushing it closed.

"Shouldn't we keep going?" the younger girl asked.

"No. I can't go any further tonight. It's too cold and I am too tired."

"Will we be safe?"

The older girl shrugged.

"I don't like that answer."

"I'm sorry, Millie. I'm just so tired. I just need to rest a while."

She shifted the bag from her shoulders and dropped it on the ground in front of her.

"I'm scared, Ally."

"We'll be fine. I promise." Ally detached the sleeping bag from the bottom of the pack and unrolled it, "We'll rest a while and move on. Just for a little while, ok?"

Millie nodded, her eyes wet with unshed tears. She pulled off her hat and a sea of dark brown curls spilled out. Ally crawled inside the sleeping bag.

"Are you tired Millie?"

Millie shook her head and looked at the door.

"We'll be fine. You keep watch for us. If you hear them coming, just wake me up and we will hide."

Ally rested her head on her arm and let her eyes close slowly. She was rapidly approaching sleep when Millie spoke again.

"What was in the box?"

Ally's eyes snapped open. She stared a moment into Millie's deep brown eyes, debating.

"I… I'm not sure."

Millie turned her attention back to the door.

"It sure was big." she muttered.

"Yes," Ally whispered, "Yes it was." She lowered her head and slipped into a dream, plagued by restless sleep.

Millie stood up and glanced around the church. She was scared, but curiosity was getting the better of her. She had the need to explore. She walked down the center aisle towards the pulpit. A memory flashed before her eyes. There Millie was, in a white dress walking down an aisle similar to this. She smiled brightly at her parents. She could see the love in their eyes.

She was yanked back into reality at the sound of a loud crack, almost like a firecracker.

Ally sat up quickly, all signs of sleep gone in a heartbeat.

"Millie? Millie, where are you?"

Millie ran down the aisle and crouched at Ally's side. Ally grabbed her tightly.

"Not a word." she said, locking her eyes to the door.

The noise came again, this time more than once in rapid succession.

"Oh god," Ally whispered as she quickly climbed out of the sleeping bag and began to roll it up.

"It's them! They found us!"

"Millie, please. Grab your hat. We have to hide." But there was no time.

The door of the church was thrown open. A figure leapt inside and quickly pushed the door shut behind him.

Outside, pounding footsteps echoed in the air.

Ally grabbed Millie's hand and darted down the aisle. She could hear the person chasing after them. She could also here the boards being yanked from the entrance.

She felt strong arms grab her from behind and pull her towards the wall. She tried to scream but a hand clamped over her mouth.

"Quiet!" the man hissed. He pushed aside a faded tapestry and pushed Ally and Millie through the doorway behind it. He followed them through and gently lowered the cloth over the doorway seconds before the main entrance was kicked open.

Millie was paralyzed with fear. She had her arms wrapped tightly around Ally's leg. She looked at the man. In the dim light it could be seen that he wasn't a man after all, but a teenage boy, his longish brown hair was pulled back into a loose ponytail. He put his finger over his lips and gave Millie a wink.

Heavy footsteps filled the church quickly. Something was shouted in a language that Ally couldn't understand. Her heart was pounding in her chest. She watched as the intruder reached behind his back and pull out a pistol.

More shouting, and as the footsteps retreated, the church entrance was pulled shut.

Realizing they were now safe, the boy lowered the gun and turned to face the girls.

"I'm sorry. I didn't know anyone would be in here."

"They…almost got us." Ally sank to her knees and began to sob.

"Look, it's okay, they didn't! We're safe."

"Why is this happening?" Ally hid her face in her hands.

Millie sat next to her and rested her head on Ally's shoulder.

"I'm Benji." he said softly. He didn't know what else to say. He sat down and leaned against the wall.

Ally looked up and wiped away her tears, "I'm Ally. This is Millie."

"Sisters?"

Ally smiled. "No, not exactly, I found her… after the… afterwards."

"She saved me." Millie said. Her voice was veiled in a deep sadness.

Benji nodded.

"I'll go." he said.

"No. Please." Ally said, "Stay here. It's not safe out there."

Benji smiled slightly.

"I'm afraid." Ally whispered.

"Me too," Benji looked down at the ground, "it will be dark soon. We can build a fire in the other room, in the corner under the hole in the ceiling. It will be a lot colder tonight."

"You've been here before?" Millie asked.

"Yeah." Benji answered as he stood up.

"Did you light the candle?"

"Yes."

"Why?" Millie looked up at him curiously.

Benji pushed aside the tapestry. He paused and glanced towards the soft glowing candle.

"Hope, I guess. Every time I look at that candle I know I am still alive."

He stepped out of the room and let the tapestry flutter down behind him.

Through the hole in the ceiling stars shimmered dimly. A thin line of smoke threaded through the hole, invisible against the black sky.

Benji, Millie, and Ally sat around the small fire, huddled close together against the cold winter air. They nibbled at sandwiches made from food Benji had taken from a nearby store. He had it hidden in a cabinet at the front of the church.

"How long have you been here?" Ally asked.

"Two weeks."

"What happened?"

"I don't really remember. It happened so fast. All I knew to do was run."

"What about your family?"

Benji stared into the fire, his eyes glossing over.

"I'm sorry, I shouldn't have asked."

"No it's ok. My story is probably the same as yours."

"How did this happen? Why didn't anyone stop them? The army...someone?"

"I don't know. I don't know anything that is going on. I had a radio but it's just static now. I'm sure if I could find a TV that worked it would be the same thing. That is if there was power anymore. From what I can tell from the radio they attacked at the same time from seemingly all directions. People said they were speaking Russian and Chinese. They came in and killed without mercy. They killed my mother and my father. I watched them put a gun to my little brother's head. I've never seen such hatred in my life. I don't understand it. I can't fathom it. But there it was, right in front of my face. They didn't see me at first. My father did. He was crying. His eyes locked with mine and in my head I heard his voice. Clearer than anything I have ever heard before. He told me to run."

Ally wiped her eyes.

"My daddy fought with them." Millie said softly, "The bad men came and he fought them. But they shot him and he is dead now. I ran with my brother but they got him to and I was by myself until Ally found me."

"Where do we go from here?" Ally asked.

"There's nowhere left to go. There's nothing left. It's gone."

"What do you mean?"

Benji did not answer. He tossed the last of his sandwich into the fire.

"I don't know why there was no one to stop them." he said, "I don't know why any of this is happening."

"It wasn't soldiers who killed my family." Ally whispered. "They came to our town. We saw them killing people and…they were doing other things to the women. My dad…he had these pills. I don't know where he got them or why he even had them. He was always paranoid about that sort of thing. It drove my mom nuts. He always looked at these conspiracy web sites and all that. But…anyway, when he saw them... when he saw what they were doing. He begged us to take this pill. He took it and my mom and older sister and her kids took it. I…I didn't. I was too scared, I was scared more of dying than facing these monsters. I watched them all die and then I ran. I was alone for a while, absolutely scared to death. A few times I wanted to just give myself to them and let it all end. What was the point? Everywhere I looked I saw death and destruction. But then, I found Millie just outside of the city. She was standing in the middle of the road staring a butterfly. She had a smile on her face. Behind her a building was burning sending this thick black smoke into the air and there she was smiling at a butterfly. She became my reason to keep going."

"And here you are." Benji said.

"Here we are."

Benji stood and walked towards his burning candle.

"I'm sleepy Ally." Millie said.

"Ok. Here, climb in the sleeping bag." Ally helped her climb in the bag, "The fire will keep you warm."

Ally rubbed Millie's hair as she fell asleep. A look of peace crossed her face, a slight smile danced across her mouth. Ally kissed her forehead and stood up. She walked to where Benji stood.

"Are you ok?"

"Not really."

"We'll be ok."

Benji was silent. He ran his finger over the flame.

"I don't think so." Benji sighed.

"Why not? We can pack up and leave in the morning; we can be out of the city by noon."

"There's nowhere to go."

"We'll find other people Benji. We'll start over. Those soldiers can't stay here forever."

"You don't understand."

"We can start over somewhere else. Somewhere they've left. We'll find more survivors."

"There are no more survivors!" Benji shouted. "There is nowhere left for us to go."

"What are you saying?"

"They've destroyed it all. America is dead, Ally. It's gone, it's been wiped away, dust, poof." Benji picked up his candle and blew it out, "There is no more hope."

Benji brushed past her and pulled open the church door. He walked outside and disappeared into the night.

Ally didn't want to think about what he said. She didn't believe it was true. There was always hope. She realized that when she found Millie.

There was always hope.

***

Benji stood in the shadows across the street from the church. He felt bad for shouting at Ally, but his fears and frustrations got the better of him. He saw the soldiers carrying a box off the truck. He knew what was inside of it. He knew what was coming. He just didn't know how to escape it.

When he went back inside the church he noticed his candle was lit again. Beside it, two more candles burned brightly. Benji watched the flickering light for a few moments before he lay down next to the dwindling fire and fell into a deep sleep.

In the morning, they woke to find three soldiers standing above them. Millie instantly began to cry. Ally grabbed her and pulled her to her chest.

"Get Up!" one spoke, barely understandable through his Russian accent.

Benji looked desperately for his gun.

He shouted again. "GET UP!"

The three of them stood up slowly.

"Please don't hurt us." Ally pleaded.

"Be quiet bitch!"

"They're going to kill us." Benji said, "We have to run."

The lead soldier cocked his head slightly. He was listening to the radio in his ear. He turned to his peers and waved them out the door. He turned back to them and grinned then lowered his weapon.

"Perhaps you prefer the bullet, no?" he said in his thick Russian accent. He laughed and ran out of the church.

"Benji what's happening? Where are they going?"

"We have to go, now!"

Above them the sound of helicopters filled the air.

"What's going on?" Ally said as she grabbed her bag.

"They're leaving."

"Leaving? Then we're safe? They're going! Why are we running?"

Benji turned to her. He placed his hands on her shoulders and looked into her eyes.

"We have to run Ally." he said more to her with his eyes.

"Oh no…" she whispered.

"We have to go now."

Millie grabbed Ally's hand and in turn Ally grabbed Benji's. Together they ran out of the church.

In the sky, dozens of helicopters roared overhead as they ran. They ran past the crumbling buildings and the burning cars. The sun was a bright beacon in the sky. They ran and they ran. Millie tripped and Ally scooped her up into her arms. Millie watched behind them as they ran. Her chin was resting on Ally's shoulder.

"Ally…" she said with a laugh in her voice, "Another sun!"

"Don't look baby. Close your eyes."

Benji looked at her and squeezed her hand tighter.

"Hope," he said to her. They ran faster.

The ground shook.

"Benji…" Ally whispered.

In the church, the three burning candles flared impossibly bright before succumbing to the coming monster. As they ran, the last burning ray of hope warming their hearts; Ally, Benji, and Millie's world ceased and the darkness overtook them.

Haven

One

It was a cool night at the end of September, the kind of night that is perfect for a couple taking a romantic stroll along the river anticipating that first kiss beneath a deep red moon. It was just such a couple that now stood beneath a dying cherry tree shivering in each others' arms. The horror of what they had witnessed was still fresh in their minds.

Cory Carr climbed out of his rundown truck and let his eyes drift to the couple. They were teenagers at most. The girl, blonde and pretty, was sobbing into her boyfriend's shoulder even as his own strong facade was at near breaking point.

"Over here, Carr." Cory moved his eyes from the couple to the gruff voice that called him. He pulled his jacket closer around him and flicked his pale hair out of his eyes. The man who called for him was Reggie Billson. He was the head man in charge of the police force around here. Cory saw his hand resting on this butt of his gun as he approached. Normally, Reggie didn't look his 39 years, but tonight, tonight his eyes looked much older.

It wasn't long before Cory saw why.

A body of a young girl, no more than 12 lay on the shore of the river, the brown water washing over her pale legs and bare feet. She wore a simple blue dress and her face appeared peaceful almost as if she were simply asleep. The wound on her throat betrayed that image. It was large and ragged, the flesh torn away to expose the large artery within. Her flesh was nearly white from lack of blood.

Cory knelt next to the body, his hands clenched into tight fists in his pockets.

"This is a problem, Carr." said Reggie again.

No kidding. Cory thought.

"This is Kelly Munson's little girl. How…just how can I explain this to her? "

"I'll do it." Cory said as he stood. He nodded to the medical examiner that immediately covered the girl with a sheet.

"I…I appreciate that Car-…Cory. I do."

"I would hold onto that appreciation sir." Cory looked past Reggie at the little girl standing next to his truck. It was the same girl, but her throat was not damaged. "She won't be the last."

***

Cory climbed into his truck and pulled the door shut. He glanced at the passenger seat and saw the girl sitting there. Her hands were neatly folded in her lap.

"Are you going to free me?" She asked and scratched her neck.

Cory closed his eyes and laid his head on the cool steering wheel.

"I'm really scared."

Just ride it out, Cory. Just ride it out.

The girl fell silent for a moment.

"Mommy, help me!" she shouted and screamed with terror.

Cory clasped his hands over his ears until the din subsided. He looked at the passenger seat. It was empty. The girl was gone. She had given him her last words and moved on to death. Cory reached into his pocket and pulled out a small notepad and a worn down pencil. He scribbled her words on the first blank sheet he came to and tossed the note book onto the seat next to him.

Cory jumped slightly when Reggie knocked on his door window. Cory cursed silently and rolled down the window.

"Is this the reason you're here?' Reggie asked point blank, "The reason you been snooping around my town for two weeks?"

"I suspect it might be, Reggie."

"You owe me an explanation son. I need to know what's happening in my town."

Cory locked eyes with Reggie. "A mother has lost her daughter. That is all you need concern yourself with. Now if you'll excuse me I have to go do your job and tell her about it."

Reggie stepped away from the truck as Cory cranked the engine.

"What are we dealing with Cory?"

Cory backed the truck up quickly throwing gravel across the cracked roadway.

"A monster, you're dealing with a monster." With that, Cory sped away.

***

The Munson house was dark when Cory pulled his truck up to the curb. He turned off the engine and sat quietly looking at the unlit windows of the small house. Reggie's words were echoing in his head. Did he owe Reggie an explanation? Reggie had allowed Cory access to the small town's records without much question and only a small bit of suspicion.

Cory had met the entire population of Haven, Montana, in the past two weeks and had even befriended a few of them. He felt as if he owed something to them. Would it be better for the town if he kept his knowledge to himself or shared it willingly?

Cory sighed and slid out of his car. He could make that decision later. Right now, he had to destroy a woman's life.

***

Reggie stormed into the police station with such force that he split the glass of the door. He marched through the lobby and into the rear of the station.

"Martha!" he shouted to the empty office.

He heard a toilet flush and a small, fat, white haired woman shuffled out of the restroom.

"Jesus Christ Reggie! Can't an old woman pop a squat for two seconds?"

"Sorry Martha. It's been a bad night. We found Callie Munson down at the river. She'd been…she's dead."

"Oh sweet Mary! That's terrible."

"Look, did you get anything on that situation I asked you about?"

"Your secret project?"

"Yeah."

Martha shuffled over to her desk and sat down with a sigh. She pulled a manila folder out of a drawer and handed it to Reggie.

"I haven't found anything on anyone named Cory Carr aged twenty-three. There's a Cory Carr aged fifty-seven born in Cratefield, Mississippi, but he's a black man."

"You found nothing?"

"Nada." Martha said as she reached for a pack of cigarettes.

"That's impossible." Reggie flipped through the file. It was page after page of negative search results in every law enforcement and government database. Not a single shred of information about Cory Carr, "We just might have ourselves a real problem here." Reggie tapped his finger on the edge of the file. He glanced at Martha and dropped the file back on her desk.

"I wouldn't get all crazy over this, Reg. He's a good kid. He's been helping out around here. Hell, he's only been here two weeks and he feels like part of the force already."

"I know that Martha, dammit. He's here two weeks and I got a dead kid on my hands. He's on his way over to Kelly's right now to tell her about her daughter."

"Why would he…" Martha stopped mid-sentence.

"I know what you're thinking. Why aren't I over there? Son of a bitch, if I don't have an answer to that question…" Reggie turned away from Martha and walked back towards the door, "I'll be on the radio if you need me."

Reggie pushed his way outside and quickly climbed into his car. He meant to get to the Munson house before Cory did any damage and he meant to get some serious answers.

***

Cory stepped onto the front porch of the Munson home and pressed his finger against the doorbell. He was about to ring when a gravelly voice sounded from behind him.

"Just what are you doing here, son?"

121

Cory dropped his arm and turned to face the man standing on the lawn. He wore a shimmering black suit and had jet black hair combed back over his head. He was a handsome man but he had an air about him. Almost as if he was artificial. Cory knew all about this man. More than he wished to know.

"Why are you here?" Cory asked, "This doesn't have anything to do with you."

"Not directly. Not yet." The man wasn't breathing. He had his hands clasped in front of him but aside from his mouth, his body was completely still.

"You promised me you wouldn't interfere."

"When my son is meddling in dangerous affairs I haven't a choice but to interfere." The man finally moved, taking several steps towards Cory.

"Leave me." Cory hissed.

"You can't help these people. They're doomed. I beg you Corrigan. Come with me away from here and let these events happen as they will."

"Don't call me that! My name is Cory."

The man looked sad for a moment. But only just, his face hardened again and he scowled at Cory.

"You shan't forget what you are, Corrigan. Your blood is my blood. You are from a Dynasty of Darkness."

"Not all of me."

The man laughed.

"This course you are on, Corrigan, will only lead to destruction. Save yourself the trouble. You'll never be one of them."

"Leave me." Cory said again.

This time, the man nodded. A pair of enormous black wings emerged from his back and embraced him. The wings combined and formed a thick heavy cloak around the man. Cory saw the glint of a silver crescent before the man was engulfed in swirling black mist and was gone.

Cory turned around. The appearance of his father did not bode well. There was something going wrong here and if his father was right, Cory would not be able to stop it.

With a sigh he knocked on the front door. It wasn't a moment before the door was opened and he was looking into the haunted and sad eyes of Kelly Munson.

Two

Cory followed Kelly down the hall to the sitting room. Kelly clicked on lights as she walked. She had been sitting in complete darkness prior to his arrival. The only light coming into the sitting room was moonlight filtering through the lace curtains covering the large picture window. Kelly sat down in a worn love seat and reached for the lamp next to her. She turned it on and rested her hands in her lap.

"I know why you're here." she said simply. She wasn't even looking at Cory, who was still standing in the entry way of the sitting room, "Reggie couldn't be bothered to come himself."

Cory was silent. He had the distinct feeling had should not have come here. He should have left this to Reggie.

"Please sit. Do you want something to drink? Tea? Water?"

Cory shook his head and sat on the edge of a flower print couch.

Kelly's eyes welled up with tears. Cory noticed they had changed from a dark blue to a bright blue grey as she began to cry. She was a young woman. Probably not even thirty yet, but she was about to receive the worst news of her life. Kelly pushed a strand of brown hair behind her ear and looked up at him.

You'll never be one of them...

"Is she dead?" she asked.

Cory nodded, "I'm very sorry."

Kelly wiped her tears away.

"She was found earlier tonight near the river. Her body was..." Cory felt his voice drop away. He didn't know how to do this.

"It's all right Cory. You can tell me." Kelly had calmed down significantly. Cory saw the light fade from her eyes.

"Her body seemed to have been...drained..." he said softly.

"Yes." Kelly whispered, "They told me that might happen."

Cory's breath caught in his throat. He was sure he didn't hear that correctly.

"I'm sorry?"

"They told me she was special and that they needed her." Kelly was crying again.

Cory felt the hairs on the back of his neck prickling.

"They promised she wouldn't be hurt. They promised I'd get her back." Kelly gestured at the lights, "That's why I had all the lights off. I was waiting for her to come back. They told me they would bring her back after I took her to them."

Are you going to free me? I'm scared! Mommy, help me!

Cory felt the air around him getting thicker. The lights flickered and dimmed.

"Who are you talking about Kelly? Who did you give Callie to?"

Kelly looked at the ceiling, "Them."

Cory looked up and saw a black mass swirling above them.

"The Shadow People." Kelly whispered.

The lights in the house exploded plunging them into darkness.

Cory leapt to his feet.

"You bastards you took my daughter from me!" Kelly was shrieking. The pitch was sending needles into Cory's ears.

Cory felt something grab onto him. In the dim moonlight he could see Kelly fighting against dark shapes.

"You promised me! You promised me she would be okay!"

Cory was yanked to his knees. He felt a hot ancient breath in his ear.

"Do not cross us." An old voice spoke, "You are safe this time because of your blood. Do not interfere again."

Cory heard a gurgling scream and felt something spray across his face.

"The betrayer is punished. Leave lest you face the same fate."

"Wha…" Cory could not finish his sentence. He felt the darkness expand around him and explode. He went crashing through the picture window and soared over the lawn. He fell hard against the road in a shower of glass. He rolled along the concrete and heard tires squealing to a stop near him.

Reggie jumped from his cruiser and ran towards Cory.

"Jesus H! What happened?" Reggie helped Cory to his feet, "You're covered in blood."

"It's not mine." Cory looked down at himself. He had several cuts on his hands, "Not all of it."

***

Cory watched as Reggie came out of the house. His face was nearly as white as Callie Munson's was down by the river. Reggie stumbled and fell to his knees, a spray of vomit bursting from his mouth. Cory looked away out of respect. No man wants to be seen on his knees puking, especially not the sheriff.

Cory didn't look up until her heard Reggie's boots crunching across glass.

"There ain't nothing left in there except blood and teeth." he said. He lurched forward and grabbed Cory by the collar, "You tell me what the fuck is happening here and you tell me right now."

Cory gently grabbed Reggie's wrists and shoved him away.

"Don't ever touch me. Ever."

Reggie rushed forward. Cory caught him by the throat and lifted him into the air. Reggie grabbed his wrist. It was like cold steel.

Cory released his grip and Reggie fell to the ground.

"I'll meet you at your office tomorrow morning. I'll tell you everything then." Cory said, and walked to his truck.

***

The hotel room was dark and quiet when Cory entered. He shut the door and secured the deadbolt as well as the security chain. He doubted they'd do much good, but it was something. He peeled off his ruined jacket and shirt and tossed them into the bathroom sink. He turned on the faucet and let the basin fill with cold water. He stared at himself in the mirror. He was pale beneath the fluorescent lights making his smooth defined chest and abdomen look slightly translucent. The small crescent birthmark on his shoulder stood out against his skin. His face was streaked with blood and his light blonde hair seemed to have a pink tint to it. He bent and cupped his hands beneath the faucet and splashed water over his face. He rubbed his hands over his cheeks. His mind was racing with the events of the day. He wasn't sure he could even comprehend what happened. It didn't seem to make much sense. Why was such a powerful force working in a small Montana town?

He straightened and watched as the water streamed down his face. For a moment it appeared as if he was crying but the water dried quickly and the illusion was gone.

126

Cory tilted his head slightly. He had heard something from the other room. It was a click and the sound of voices.

The television.

Cory stepped slowly out of the bathroom and peaked around the corner to the main room. A young man was sitting on the edge of the bed watching Oprah Winfrey give a young woman a car. The man had large white wings and was dressed in simple white linen clothes. He was thin but muscular and had dark brown hair that barely touched the tops of his ears.

"Can't you put those things away?" Cory asked.

The young man looked at him and smirked. The wings folded and disappeared inside two flaps on the man's back. The only sign they had ever been there were the two slits in the linen shirt he wore.

"The rest of the flock must be jealous of that skill." Cory said as he sat down in a chair near the bed.

"Perks of being half human I guess," he said and tossed the remote onto the bed, "By the way, flock? We're not birds, Cory."

Cory simply shrugged and watched the man. His name was Jeremiah Prince. He was the son of a rogue angel named Plas and a human woman named Kara. She died in childbirth and the only way Jeremiah had ever known her was by turning his back on his father and dedicating himself to the Order of Angels. They now lunch every Thursday in a place Cory could only dream of entering.

Cory was of the dark breed and therefore not allowed to enter the great kingdom above. Further complicating matters was the fact that Cory and Jeremiah had been lovers for the last two years. At least until Cory took it upon himself to flee to Earth for reasons even he isn't sure of yet.

Jeremiah's blue eyes twinkled, "You could have said goodbye."

"I'm sorry. I didn't want you in any danger."

"Shouldn't that have been my decision?" Jeremiah turned on the bed so he was sitting across from Cory, "Shouldn't you have at the very least told me you were going?"

Cory scoffed, "I doubt your boss would let you come down with your dark breed boyfriend."

Jeremiah looked down at his hands, "I don't like it when you refer to yourself like that."

Cory didn't answer. Instead he asked a question that had been nagging him since he saw Jeremiah sitting on the bed.

"Why did they send you?"

Jeremiah looked up quickly, unable to control the look of shock on his face. He had never been any good at masking his feelings, especially when it came to Cory.

"Dammit, Jer." Cory stood up.

Jeremiah stood as well. He rushed over to Cory.

"They only wanted me to deliver a message."

"Do they know about us?"

"I don't know. All I know is that they came to me in secret and sent me in secret. Something bad is happening Cory. It's something that was not in the Scrolls of Parasi."

The Scrolls of Parasi were ancient angelic prophecies that were to have foretold all the major events in both the spirit and earthly realms. They are not something Cory had ever expected to have brought up in his travels. In fact, none of this is what he was expecting.

"I don't understand what this has to do with me." Cory said even though he had his suspicions.

"The Order wants me to help you investigate claims of certain Underland activities on earth."

"Underland activities, so, some bad mojo brewing in Hell these days?" Cory asked with a thick layer of sarcasm.

"We don't exactly know what is happening."

Cory again had his suspicions that whatever The Order was worried about was taking place right here in Haven.

"Is that everything?" Cory asked, "Any other pearls of knowledge for me?"

Jeremiah shook his head.

The two were silent for a moment. Jeremiah looked at the floor as if he were ashamed to meet Cory's eyes.

"You've been gone so long..." he whispered.

Cory stepped forward and kissed Jeremiah. He couldn't resist the urge any longer. Together they stepped back and collapsed in a mass of limbs upon the bed. They devoured each other for hours and eventually fell asleep in each others' arms. They did not wake again until morning.

Three

Reggie had been sitting in his office since dawn. He had hardly slept a wink all night and was eagerly watching the clock. It had just clicked past 10am. Reggie was getting concerned. Cory should have been here by now. Maybe he fled? He could have shred that poor woman to pieces and took off for parts unknown. He should go find him. Yeah. He should do that. Reggie pushed back in his chair and stood up. It was a useless motion. Cory was standing in the door to his office.

"I apologize. I should have been here earlier."

Feeling foolish now, Reggie sat down. He gestured for Cory to do the same. Cory closed the office door and sat down across from him.

"You uh..." Reggie couldn't seem to get the words to form and his neck had started throbbing. He rubbed his hands over it and realizing what he was doing, folded them on the desk.

"I am sorry about that." Cory said, "I didn't mean to…"

"Look uh Cory. Mr. Carr. I just want to know what you know. I got people dying in my town and I got you, a stranger, all up in it."

"Let me start then with my full name. It is Corrigan Carrion." Cory rested his hands in his lap and stared into Reggie's eyes, "The rest of this will be hard to believe."

Reggie leaned back in his chair.

Cory was having an extreme amount of difficulty putting this into words. He sighed and decided to just blurt it out.

"I'm not entirely human."

Reggie blinked.

"I'm half human to be exact."

Reggie was glad his gun was strapped to his hip.

"What is your other half then?" He asked.

"Reaper."

"Pardon?"

"Reaper, grim or otherwise, you know, Death. My Father is Death."

Reggie felt his mouth go dry. He was dealing with a certified loon.

"Are you on drugs?"

"No." Cory shook his head, "I'm not."

"You come into my town and it's not a week before a little girl and her mother are killed and then you tell me you're the son of the grim reaper? I have half a mind to toss you into a cell."

"You can do that if you want. It won't hold me."

"This is a fuck and a half right here."

"Look, Reggie…"

"You can call me Sheriff Billson. I'll be goddamned if I'll be on a first name basis with a crackpot lunatic."

"These murders will not stop, you can think me as crazy as you want to Reggie, but these murders will not stop."

"What can you do?"

"What?"

"If you're part death you should have powers right? Can you touch someone and they die?"

"No. I am not entirely sure what I can do."

"Bull shit."

Cory looked up at him.

"Alright I can make people do things. Make them trust me without ever knowing me. Make them let a complete stranger help out on the police force. You know that sort of thing."

Reggie blinked. Suddenly, things were making sense. Reggie was unsure as to why he was letting Cory get so close to police business and investigations. Now he knew.

"Are you a god fearing man, Reggie?"

"What the hell does that have to do with anything?"

Cory shrugged slightly.

"Shouldn't you know that anyway?" Reggie asked with a scoff.

"I'm not psychic if that's what you think. I do have some knowledge about things."

Reggie was becoming steadily uncomfortable.

"Your wife…" Cory began.

"Don't you dare mention her, you hear me? Not a word."

Cory nodded.

"You should rethink where you place your blame. Not everything is under His control. Not anymore." Cory lowered his head, "Sometimes someone wants something that is forbidden and it is snatched away without thought or reason. Not in the human sense at least."

"I don't want to hear this."

"You may not want to, but you need to. Not hearing the truth will prevent you from being of any use to your town if I'm right about what I believe is happening. You need to understand that everything you believe, everything you were taught, is wrong."

"She was murdered. I was on a case and someone broke into the apartment and murdered her."

"Ryan Setnaro."

"How…never mind. Yes, that was the guy. We caught him. He swore up and down he didn't do it."

"He didn't."

"He videotaped it."

"If you can believe for a moment that what I told you is true, then perhaps you can believe the truth about your wife. She was not killed by Ryan Setnaro. Not exactly anyway, she was killed by a Zar."

"I don't need to hear this."

"You do. You will. The Zar are a race of demons from the Underland. More specifically, Zarlaya. They are fascinated by humans. They hate them. They envy them. But worst of all they desire them. One of them desired your wife. He took over the body of Ryan Setnaro and he desecrated her. He destroyed her utterly."

Reggie's eyes welled with tears.

"You need to know this because you need to realize that true evil exists in this world and others. Your wife was stolen from you in the worst way imaginable. You cannot get her back but it is not God's fault. It is not your fault. When a Zar wants a human, it will take it."

"I don't believe this."

"Then I will show you."

Cory leapt forward and grabbed Reggie's hand. The world around them seemed to bend and darkness swallowed everything.

Reggie had squeezed his eyes shut the second the world started to go weird. He now opened them slowly. He stood on a vast stone mesa. Spread out below him was the vastness of Underland. He saw large buildings and keeps spread out across the rocky landscape. In the distance, the sky was red and smokey. Small black shapes flew through the air.

"Is this Hell?" Reggie stammered.

"No. That over there is Hell." Cory pointed to the red portion of sky, "This is a small part of Underland. This is where the dark breeds reside. Demons, Reapers, and others not of your world or The Light."

"Why are you showing me this?"

"I'm showing you this because I need your help." Cory pointed to a dark spire far in the distance, "That is the gate to Zarlaya, home of the Zar. I think they are responsible for the deaths in Haven."

"Can we stop them?"

Another voice answered him, "I'm reasonably sure that you cannot do anything to the Zar, mortal."

Cory and Reggie both turned. Cory grimaced at the site of his father standing there again in his black suit.

"You brought a human to the Underland, Corrigan. This is expressly forbidden. There are laws that must be followed. Your unique position does not grant you immunity from them."

"Is this…" Reggie's eyes widened.

"I needed to show him."

"Enough is enough of these games, Corrigan! You've gone

much too far now. Take the human back and leave his town. It is not our place to meddle in human affairs. It is time for you to come home and learn the ways of the Carrion Clan."

"No. And my name is Cory."

Death rushed forward and grabbed Cory by his collar. He shook him violently.

"Do not assume that because you are my son that you have some type of protection from me, boy. If I desire it you will come home. You'd also do well to realize that nothing you do in this world or the other is in secret. There are no secrets, Corrigan. You will return this…human…to his place and return to my side."

"Get your hands off me, Father." Cory pushed his father away, "I am not part of your clan. I have work I must do and you shall not interfere with that work."

"I know what you are trying to do, what He promised you. You're going to get yourself destroyed, Corrigan. I can't protect you for long."

Reggie's eyes darted between the two of them.

"I don't want your protection." Cory grabbed Reggie again and they both vanished.

Death lowered his head.

"If only that were true." he whispered.

Four

The sun was bright in the sky causing Kevin West to squint as he rode his bike across the park. The park was strangely empty today. Normally, it would be crawling with kids and parents spending some precious afternoon time together.

Kevin steered his bike around the playground towards the

street that led home. He felt something tug at his shirt and glanced over his shoulder.

His eyes widened in terror at the visage floating behind him. It had a pale white face shrouded in dark wispy robes. It's teeth where yellowed and long with flecks of red on the enamel. Kevin felt his heart lurch in his chest and the roots of his hair instantly streaked white. He felt the cold scaly hands grabbing him and lifting him right from his bike. He tried to scream but a clammy hand closed over his mouth. He was pulled into the air. He saw his bike rolling along the grass before it finally fell over.

It would be the last thing Kevin would ever see. His world fell into darkness and he knew no more.

***

Three other children of Haven vanished that day.

Reggie sat in his office with his face in his hands. His mind was awash with thoughts of hell and disappearing children.

Cory sat across from him silently contemplating the events. He would let Reggie think and knew it was best not to try to interject his own beliefs as to what was happening. It was enough that he had taken him to the Underland. A weaker human would have been driven mad by what they saw. Reggie it seemed was handling it remarkably well.

"I need for you to leave now Cory. I have four missing children to find."

Cory nodded, "I would find their parents. They'll more than likely be in…"

"I appreciate your desire to assist in an ongoing police investigation, Cory." Reggie said, cutting him off, "Unfortunately, you're not a police officer. We'll handle it. You'd do best to go back to your hotel. Maybe you'll think it wise to pack up and move on."

Cory blinked. Perhaps Reggie didn't handle the recent revelations as well as he thought.

Reggie looked up at him.

Cory stood, his face reddening with anger, "You're making a mistake."

"Noted." Reggie said.

Cory leaned forward and whispered to Reggie, "They're already dead, Reggie. Don't waste the time when you can prevent more bloodshed."

"Get out of my office." Reggie snarled this order and slowly rose out of his chair, "I want you out of Haven. If I see you again Cory…God help you and what you brought to my town."

Cory turned away and walked out of the office.

Reggie slunk back into his chair. His sanity wouldn't let him accept what he had witnessed and learned. He would explain it as a hallucination, anything to discount what he had seen. He hadn't been taken to some other dimension. He hadn't seen Death arguing with his son. He had missing children to find and he'd be damned if he let some crackpot lunatic trick him into believing this madness.

He wouldn't believe it. He sat there for a few moments trying to convince himself not to.

At least not until Kevin West walked into the police station. He had a gaping wound on his chest and blood streaming from his eyes.

"Sheriff!" Martha shouted.

Reggie stood up and saw Kevin through the glass door of his office.

"Jesus and Mary…" he whispered and rushed out of the room, "Get an ambulance over here, Martha."

Martha simply stood looking at Kevin.

136

"Martha, now!"

She shook her head to clear her thoughts and darted for the phone.

Reggie crouched next to Kevin and wiped some of the blood off his face, "You'll be okay son."

Kevin looked up into Reggie's face. His eyes were glassy and dim.

"They're everywhere." he said and fainted.

***

Cory burst into his hotel room and slammed the door shut behind him. The crash of the door echoed through his room and rang in his ears. He was furious with Reggie. To completely turn his back on everything Cory had shown him, it was maddening. Cory had risked a lot taking Reggie to the Underland. He'd been discovered doing so and now Reggie was ignoring it all. His thoughts were roaring with rage loudly enough that he hardly heard the phone on the small bedside table ringing.

He moved to answer it when the hotel door burst open and Jeremiah rushed in.

"Where have you been?" He rushed over and grabbed Cory's hand. "We have to go now. I found someone who needs to speak with you."

The ringing phone forgotten, Cory allowed Jeremiah to lead him out of the room.

***

She figured it was the boots that were freaking the locals out. Maybe it was her spiky pink hair. Surely they'd seen pink hair before. Maybe it was the leather pants or the metal studded fingerless gloves she wore.

She walked up to the counter of the run down gas station and dropped a bottle of Diet Coke on the cracked Formica.

The clerk stared at her.

"How much?" she asked.

"You…you got horns." the clerk said.

So that was it then. She always seemed to forget she had them. They weren't even that big. It wasn't as if they were huge curved monstrosities. On the contrary, they were small nubs about an inch or so tall. They did have the slightest curve and point to them. They always seemed to put people off.

"Costume party." she mumbled, "How much for the coke?"

"A dolla." The clerk was still staring at her horns.

"Take a picture asshole." She tossed a buck on the counter and walked out.

Ah, the life of a half-demon.

The young woman mounted her motorcycle and put her helmet on. She revved the engine a few times and roared away from the gas station.

She was more annoyed than usual when this sort of thing happened. In most cases she just ignored it. This time however, she felt hurt. If they knew why she was here they'd look at her differently.

She hunkered down and sped up the cycle. Her trip to Haven was already off to a rocky start. She'd have to put that behind her if she wanted to succeed. She was here to save the town from destruction and she meant to do just that. Come Hell or high water. Truth be told, she only expected Hell.

***

Cory followed Jeremiah into the dark warehouse. He could see the empty skeletons of tall racks and storage areas surrounding the huge empty main floor. He felt increasingly apprehensive about coming here. Jeremiah didn't have many details about who they were meeting or why, and the dark desolate meeting place wasn't doing much for Cory's nerves.

"I don't suppose there are any lights here?" Cory mumbled. Before he could move to investigate the lack of lights, a bright red flame exploded in the center of the room. The flame flashed brightly and dissipated leaving a disgusting looking demon in its place. He was of medium height, with squat goat legs and a fat drooping belly. He wore a dark red vest that barely covered his ample bosom. He had long shaggy fur running out of his ears and two long curling horns on the top of his head. The left horn was broken off half way through and gave him a slightly uneven appearance. The demon looked at them with his face folded in disgust. He hacked a large wad of gunk from his chest and spat it to the ground. The blob sizzled against the concrete floor.

"Someone wanna tell me what the flying fiddly fuck I'm doin' here?" His voice was deep and sounded like he was talking through a bubble of the gunk he just spat out.

The demon's stench had reached Cory's nose. He felt like he might be sick.

The demon shuffled forward, his hooves clacking against the concrete. He sniffed the air.

"You two are half-breeds."

Cory scowled. The demon rested his eyes on him. It was but a moment before they widened and he stumbled backwards.

"No...no..." The demon spun around and ran back towards the portal he came through. He was digging into a pouch that hung at his side.

Jeremiah stepped forward and spoke. The voice that came from his mouth was not his own. It echoed through the warehouse with power and vibrated the windows in their frames.

"I am an Emissary of the Light. You will stop and face me."

The demon skidded along the floor. Cory could see his body shaking in terror. He wanted nothing more than to flee.

"Turn and face me Jacobi."

The demon, Jacobi, turned slowly. His eyes were wide with terror.

Cory glanced at Jeremiah and at once saw why the demon was so afraid. Jeremiah was engulfed in white flames. His wings were fully spread behind him. His beauty was terrifying. Cory almost fell to his knees in awe.

"You will tell us the Tale, Jacobi."

Cory saw a stream of urine running along the floor.

"Jere…" Cory was silenced by a glare from Jeremiah.

"I…I thought you types didn't believe in the demon tales." Jacobi stammered.

"Only The Tale of the Three."

"It's just a legend, it's nothing to worry you or your master about."

"TELL ME!" Jeremiah's voice exploded in the air, shattering the windows and showering glass upon them.

Cory felt a sliver slice through his cheek. A thin stream of blood streaked down towards his jaw line.

"The legend speaks of three mix bloods that will stand against the coming darkness and battle a demon army. They are of the blood of the Three Houses of Afterworld and the blood of Earthworld."

The Three Houses of Afterworld, Cory thought, *Angels, Demons, and Reapers.*

"It is said the precursor to the Demon Army is the resurrection of the fourth house." Jacobi lowered his head when he said this but he was not finished, "The legend says the Lord of the Dead will unite with the Darkest Tribe and bring rise to the Fourth House and thus begin the Apocalypse. The end times of the Earthworld. The fall of God and Church; the return of the Father of Deceit and the return of Lord Lucifer, Master of Hell and rightful Ruler of the Underland."

Jacobi had lost his fear now. He looked at Cory and Jeremiah with a grin on his face. Cory felt his head spinning. His knees were going weak. He was partly aware of the loud roaring sound coming from outside of the warehouse.

He knew that the Darkest Tribe of the Underland was the old time name for the Zar. This legend was coming to pass. The Zar were working towards some goal here in Haven.

"Cory?" Jeremiah was looking at him, his glowing white fire gone now. His wings had returned to the slits in his back.

The Lord of the Dead will unite with the Darkest Tribe.

The Lord of the Dead will unite with the Zar.

"What have you done?" Cory whispered. He could hear Jacobi cackling nearby.

The Lord of the Dead… Cory's Father.

Five

Reggie stood in the dim hallway of the hospital looking through the wired glass at a comatose boy with a look of pure terror on his face. Even unconscious the fear that Kevin had felt was evident.

Reggie wiped his hands across his face. He was on the verge of a breakdown. He could feel it. His mind was going to crack under the truth of what was happening in his town. Events he was completely powerless to stop, assuming he could even think up a way to attempt to stop them. He figured his best chance was to track down Cory, who for some reason had neglected answering or returning his calls. To emphasize his frustration, he pulled out his cell phone for the fifth time and checked the screen for any missed calls or messages. There were none.

The lights in the hallway flickered slightly.

Reggie returned his phone to his pocket and felt the hairs on his neck and arms abruptly stand straight up. He glanced down the hall as several alarms started going off.

"What the hell..."

Several nurses were running down the hall and into various rooms.

"Oh my Jesus!" A young nurse, who Reggie remembered flirting with a few days ago at the bar across town, stepped out of a patient's room. She was covered in blood.

Reggie moved towards her but stopped when he caught movement out of the corner of his eye. He saw Kevin sitting up in his bed. Reggie was vaguely aware of another nurse darting past him completely covered in blood and gore but his attention was focused on Kevin. The boy was staring intently at him. Kevin raised his hand and pointed and unleashed a scream so terrible that Reggie felt his bladder release.

It was only a second later that the window was useless. Kevin's body had simply burst and his insides coated the hospital room like freshly covered paint. The window Reggie had been looking through was coated with a curtain of blood.

Reggie watched as Kevin's eyeball slid down the glass, rolling as if trying to have a last look at the world.

Above him, Reggie saw thick black shapes flying through the air. They all had long curved blades. He watched as one swooped down and tore into one of the nurses. Her stomach contents spilled out onto the floor mixing with the rapidly growing river of blood flowing from the rooms.

"Hail Mary full of grace…" One of the shapes slowed and turned to him. It had a gash of a mouth filled with rotted, yet somehow still sharp teeth.

"It sees us." the creature hissed.

Reggie felt something inside him slip. He was done now. He turned and ran.

***

Cory stepped into his hotel room. Jeremiah was right behind him.

"What if he is wrong?" Jeremiah asked, "He's a demon, he could be lying."

"A demon commanded by an Emissary of God cannot lie." Cory walked over to his phone. For a moment he thought he felt the ground shake but dismissed it. He scooped up the received and dialed for messages.

"He said other things…"Jeremiah began, but was cut off by Cory.

"They found the boy who disappeared. I have to go." Cory dropped the receiver. It bounced off the cradle and fell to the floor. He walked to the door and pulled it open.

Jeremiah moved to follow him but Cory stopped him.

"I need you to stay here."

"No."

"Please, just trust me. I'm afraid something will happen to you. Please wait for me here."

"What about the Tale of the Three?" Jeremiah asked, "We should be doing this together."

"There are only two of us in case you didn't notice and how can we be sure that even is about us?"

Cory knew his argument was foolish. There were no other mix bloods alive besides Cory, Jeremiah, and the apparent half demon. Cory was going to attempt to plead his case further when his vision blurred and a blood curdling scream exploded in his head. He grabbed his head and fell to his knees. A thin stream of blood poured from his nose.

"Cory?" Jeremiah rushed over and knelt next to him, "What happened?"

The hotel room was gone. Cory could only see a dim hospital corridor filled with black shapes and a river of blood. At the end of the hall Cory saw his Father laughing as a rush of small white orbs swirled in the air around him. Each one disappeared inside his chest. His father stopped laughing and seemed to look directly at Cory.

The vision vanished and Cory found himself back in his hotel room. He was in Jeremiah's arms.

"You were screaming." Jeremiah whispered.

Cory realized he was covered in sweat and his heart was pounding in his chest.

"It's started." he said softly, "It's already started."

"What's started?" A female voice asked.

Cory and Jeremiah looked up at the young woman standing in the doorway. She had spiked pink hair and a small hoop nose ring. Cory immediately noticed the horns jutting out of her forehead.

"Who are you?" he asked as he stood.

She responded with some type of guttural speech that neither Jeremiah nor Corey understood.

"Alice for short." she said.

"You're half demon." Jeremiah nudged Cory.

"However did you know?" Alice asked. She stepped past them and sat down on Cory's bed. She set her motorcycle helmet on the floor between her heavy black boots and looked up at them.

"Well?" she asked.

Cory and Jeremiah looked at each other.

"You were about passed out when I got here. Care to explain that?"

"I'll have to show you." Cory took Jeremiah's hand and held his other hand out to Alice. She took it and in a blink they were gone.

He took them to the hospital. It didn't much resemble a hospital on the outside. It was a one story building with nondescript glass doors that lead into an empty waiting room. They walked in slowly and Jeremiah pointed to a directory near the door.

"They built down?" he wondered aloud. The directory showed four sub levels. One labeled surgery, one labeled radiology and labs, the last two labeled morgue and storage. The main floor was for recovery and offices. An unusual set up but Cory figured it must work for a small town.

"Why are we here?" Alice asked.

"He was here." Cory answered.

"Who was?"

Cory walked towards a set of double doors.

"Do you smell that?" Jeremiah sniffed the air.

Cory knew what he smelled. He pressed a button next to the doors and they opened slowly.

The right hand door stopped midway. Its progress blocked by a body.

The left side however revealed the massacre that lay inside.

The smell of blood increased drastically and Cory found himself barely able to suppress the urge to vomit.

"Who did this?" Alice whispered.

"The Zar," Cory let the doors shut, "and my Father."

Cory knew searching the hospital would be a waste of time. Anyone in this building would be dead. He now had no idea where to go from here, or how to stop whatever it was that his father was planning.

"Why would he kill these people? What is he trying to do?"

Cory looked at Alice.

"He took their souls. He's feeding on them." he explained."A Reaper's job is to usher the souls of the recently departed to their afterlife. There was a legend among us that a Grim, the leader of the Reapers, would become a Soul Eater. One who gained power from devouring human souls in order to start The New Age."

"What is The New Age?" Jeremiah asked.

"They say it's the time when Reapers would rule Earth." Cory sat down in one of the waiting room chairs, "I always thought it was just a story. The Soul Eater can't be real but in that vision I saw, there were souls entering my father's body."

"Why would the Zar unite with your father to usher in a new age of reaper rule?" Alice asked, "What's in it for them?"

"Jacobi said they were trying to bring back the Fourth House." Jeremiah said.

Alice arched her eyebrows, "You spoke with Jacobi?"

"Yes. He told us the Tale of the Three."

Alice paled.

"You're both mix bloods?"

"I thought you knew that." Cory said, "I'm half Reaper. Jeremiah is half Angel."

"Jacobi lied to you." Alice stated.

"Impossible. I am an Emissary of..."

"Tell me, why would a demon care if you were sent from the

high holy one or not? He has no power over Demons, contrary to popular belief. Do you two know anything?"

Cory lowered his head. He was becoming more and more confused. If his father had become the Soul Eater, why would he be trying to return the Fourth House?

"The Fourth House is not the house of Lucifer the man. Lucifer, as you clearly understand it, was The Devil who ruled over Hell. He died centuries ago which ushered in the various Houses of the Underland. His name however became more than a name. It is a title. The Fourth House is also known as The One House. The ruler of that house is called Lucifer."

Cory looked at Alice, "Then what is The One House?"

Jeremiah leapt to his feet.

"I have to go." he said, "I'll be back." His wings burst from his back and wrapped around him. He was gone in a flash of light.

"I think your boyfriend knows what it means."

Cory shot a look at her, "Why don't you fill me in."

She gave a look as though she was indulging the request of a child, or music student who'd never heard of punk rock. "According to the real prophecy three mix bloods will band together to stop the rise of the Fourth House. Just like Jacobi told you. What he neglected to mention was that he who raises the Fourth House will be Lucifer, Lord of The One House, Ruler of Dark Breeds. 'And he so shall be named Lucifer and his power will bring the end upon Earthworld and The One House will rise from its ash.' That's a direct quote. It means that the Dark Breeds will rise up under a new Lucifer and turn Earth into The One House."

Cory was beginning to understand.

"Your Father isn't planning some Reaper Renaissance and he isn't trying to resurrect Lucifer..."

"He's trying to become him." Cory finished her sentence. It

was falling into place now. Unfortunately, he didn't have much time to dwell on the issue. A large explosion filled the air. The dark sky flared orange and the ground trembled.

"There's another part of the prophecy." Alice said, ignoring the explosion.

Cory stood and walked to a nearby window.

"There must be a willing sacrifice in the name of the one who will be Lucifer. A big one."

"What does that mean?"

"It means a whole lotta people must sacrifice themselves."

A low rumble led to another explosion.

"What the hell is happening out there?" Cory asked.

"They're killing themselves, Cory."

It was true. Cory looked out the window and saw deep orange glow at the horizon. If it weren't past nightfall he'd of thought it was dawn.

"No…" Corey whispered. He felt a deep pain in his chest. He had failed.

Haven was burning.

Six

Reggie stood amongst a sea of people. They were walking with torches in one hand and in some cases holding their children in the other. He didn't know where they were going or why they were setting fire to the town and nothing he said seemed to stop them. They simply walked past him, expressionless and unblinking. Something seemed to have taken over everyone in the town and whatever or whoever was responsible was forcing them to burn everything in their path.

He recognized the faces as they past. These were his friends, his colleagues, his neighbors. All mindlessly walking towards something, some ending he was reasonably sure would be close at hand.

He was broken. His mind and spirit were shattered. He watched the people he had sworn to protect march past him. They were under some kind of spell, and only then did he realize the depth of his failure. An entire town of people was walking towards their inevitable slaughter and destruction. Reggie watched as Mario Contellio kicked his foot through the front glass window of Amy's Antiques, and tossed his torch inside.

Reggie began to recite The Lord's Prayer. His words whispered through his lips and disappeared under the thump of hundreds of feet pounding the blacktop.

He let his eyes rise towards the sky and was horrified by what he saw. A swirling sea of demonic shapes dipped and soared through the air. These were different from the ones at the hospital, more grotesque, more terrifying. He ripped his gun from its holster and fired rounds into the sky. They did no damage of course. In fact, the bullets only seemed to enrage one of the monsters. It looked down at him with two fat moist heads that sat atop its round torso. They both looked at Reggie and after a moment of clicky communication, it swept down towards him.

Reggie fired the last remaining bullets in his gun. They bounced harmlessly off the monsters thick leathery chest. Reggie lowered his gun and watched as the monster flew towards him. He saw the shimmery red stained teeth in both of its impossibly large mouths. He saw the jagged claws on both of the creature's hands.

In the moment before he thought his body would be torn in two, he saw an arm reach out and catch the beast by the throat, and with strength betraying the figure's size, throw the demon to the ground.

"They're not nearly as heavy as they look." Cory said as he jerked his arm and snapped the demon's neck. Its other head moaned in grief. Cory dispatched that one as well, "They're kind of like birds, very brittle. They're strong but it doesn't take much to hurt them."

"I…I shot it."

"Human weapons don't usually work, at least not guns."

Reggie looked at Cory saw the sadness in his eyes, despite his attempts to hide it.

"Can you stop this?" Reggie asked, "Can you save them?"

"Where are they going?" Cory asked, ignoring his questions.

"The gas plant, it supplies gas to the entire town." The ground shivered again, "I think they're blowing the tanks. Jesus Christ, if they blow the lines this entire town will be destroyed."

Cory watched the sea of people walking aimlessly around him. He heard an engine roar as Alice rode through the people. By some miracle, she managed to avoid hitting anyone.

Reggie stumbled backwards when he saw her.

"Yeah, I have horns. Get over yourself." She turned to Cory, "This is insane. How is your father strong enough to influence this many people?"

Suddenly, everyone stopped. They all lowered their torches to the ground and looked up at the sky.

"Oh no…" Cory whispered, "Get me to the gas plant now. Reggie, you need to get out of here."

"I'm not leaving these people."

"If I can't stop this…"

Reggie simply nodded his head. He understood the consequences.

Cory climbed on the back of the motorcycle and Alice kicked it into gear. Cory looked at Reggie as they sped off. There was a dull grey glow around his body. It was the same aura that surrounded all of the people kneeling around them. It was a marker. Cory was horrified to see it and by what it meant. All of these people were marked for death. He silently pleaded for Alice to go faster.

There is a moment before everything in the world seems to go wrong where time seems to slip into a slow motion slideshow. For Cory, that happened when he saw Jeremiah flying through the army of demons overhead. He watched as Jeremiah effortlessly turned and spun his way around the grotesque creatures that snapped and snarled at him.

Jeremiah swooped down towards the motorcycle.

Cory heard him call his name clearly despite the thunder of the burning buildings around them. He heard the sound of the scythe slicing into Jeremiah's body even clearer.

Cory's father floated in the air behind Jeremiah gripping his weapon tightly. He looked down at Cory and shook Jeremiah free of his blade. He fell lifelessly and hit the ground just feet in front of the bike. Cory heard Alice curse and jerk the bike to the side. It tilted and spilled them both to the road and skittered in a shower of sparks, slamming into several people until it came to a stop.

Cory leapt to his feet and ran to Jeremiah. His cheek was a river of dark blood. His once vibrant blue eyes now were fading and weak.

"Co...ry..."

"No Jer...Don't talk. Alice! Help me!" Cory turned back to Jeremiah, "Don't say anything you'll be fine."

"Listen. This...is fated. You have to go."

"Please hold on Jeremiah. Please." Cory could not hold back his tears. They ran freely down his cheeks. He saw them drip on Jeremiah's lips, "Please...don't leave me. I can't do this without you."

Jeremiah smiled slightly, "I love you, Cory."

Cory's father slowly lowered himself to the ground. He was impeccably dressed as always. His black suit showed not a drop of the blood he had freed from the body of his son's lover. His scythe scratched the pavement, sparking slightly, "There will be a cleansing fire and this land will be scorched pure."

Cory leaned forward and kissed Jeremiah. Alice had made her way over and crouched beside them. Cory looked at her, "Stay with him." He stood slowly and turned to his father.

"It's time to come home, Corrigan."

Cory clenched his fists and rushed forward. He threw himself at his father and their battle began.

Jeremiah looked over at Alice, "Please protect him. You and Cory must make it out of here. Your destiny demands…" His eyes closed for a moment and Alice believed he was gone. But Jeremiah was not finished, "Listen to me Alice. The Three…I am not one of you. There is another." He pulled her close to him and with his last breaths he told her all that he knew.

Cory hit the ground hard. His nose shattered and his body weakened. His father was so fast. He could do nothing to stop him.

"You are not a failure, Corrigan. You tried. How could you know? I am the Grim now. In moments I will be Lucifer. The Fourth House, The One House will be risen and I will rule. You can rule at my side."

Cory wiped blood from his mouth.

"You are an abomination." he said and his father laughed.

"I am an abomination? You are the one who defiled yourself with that…creature. I destroyed it and saved you from his influence. You belong with us in the dark, boy. There is no future for you in the light. There is no future for Light at all."

"I loved him and you took him away."

"The cost of living among them is losing what you care about Corrigan. Filth begets filth."

"I am going to destroy you." Cory said his voice thick with fury. From behind them came a low whoosh and thud sound.

"Not today." his father said.

The roar of a motorcycle briefly overpowered the sound of the gas plant beginning to explode. Alice reached out and grabbed Cory. She yanked him onto the back of the bike without slowing. She quickly spun the bike around and slammed on the gas. The bike shot forward and blew past Cory's father. He stood laughing as the world exploded around him.

The gas plant erupted in a fireball. The ground shook violently as the gas mains beneath the streets caught fire and exploded. Cory and Alice were seconds ahead of the blasts. Cory glanced over his shoulder and saw Jeremiah for the final time lying among the citizens of Haven. They were all reaching towards the heavens and crying, not in fear or pain, but joy. His father had corrupted them completely. He watched as the flames claimed his lover's body and then he turned and buried his face in Alice's back. He cried as Haven's ashes rained down around them.

As the flames devoured Haven, Reggie stood suspended in time. He had a smile on his face as he watched his wife stepping towards him. She reached her hand to him and he smiled as the last of the gas lines ignited and the violent flames consumed him.

Epilogue

Cory stood on the side of the road. He and Alice had traveled over a hundred miles from Haven, yet the glow of the fire was still visible and the ash continued to fall. His tears had dried yet his heart was still in pain. He figured that was something he would live with from now on.

Alice approached him and placed a hand on his shoulder.

"We should go."

"Where do angels go when they die?" Cory asked softly.

"I wish I knew."

"I wish I knew too." Cory turned to her, "You can go without me."

"We have to stay together…"

"I'll find you soon. Just…I need to go now. Alone."

"We didn't fail Cory. You did not fail."

"That town is gone now. Those people…"

"Jeremiah told me it was supposed to happen. The Three were not supposed to stop this from happening. Our time is later."

"There is no Three. Jeremiah is dead."

"He wasn't one of us. He told me…"

"He was half human, half angel. He was one of us."

"There is another. One who is not human. One who is of both Light and Dark."

"What does that mean?"

"Jeremiah said the third is half-angel half-reaper. He also said it was your brother."

Cory's eyes widened. Was it possible? A brother? Had his father mated with an Angel? He considered them to be filth, almost as bad as humans. He didn't know how to process this. It was mind boggling.

Alice climbed on her bike.

"Get on, Cory."

"I…I'll find you, Alice. Please go without me."

"Jeremiah asked me to promise to protect you. If I let you go on your own I will be breaking that promise."

Cory simply looked at the dirt.

Alice kick started the bike, "I was never good at keeping promises anyway."

With a wave she sped off.

Cory watched as she disappeared in a cloud of dust. He was alone now. His life profoundly changed. His grief insurmountable, his destiny lay ahead but he felt no urgency in following it. He had lost the one he loved and now learned he had a brother somewhere. He was lost and knew to do only one thing.

He would wander until he found his way again.

The Book of Names

PENETRATION.

That word is what helped Beauford Bixby get through each miserable day of his life. Penetration. The anticipation of it kept him from driving the putty knife he was currently using through his throat. Knowing that high end cunt was waiting for him locked up tight as Fort Knox in his basement made his heart beat faster. His mouth watered at the thought of it. Penetration. He barely caught himself before he started to moan. Already his penis was hardening, although one wouldn't know it as his ample gut prevented any show and tell.

Beauford scraped the last of the crusty paint from the wall and tossed the putty knife aside. Six months in this shit hole, breathing in pounds of asbestos and lead. It was a wonder he hadn't dropped dead already, and with his luck he probably had a two pound tumor taking up residence somewhere in his body. He figured as much with the blackouts and his new hobby. Maybe they were related.

Then again, maybe not. Maybe his new hobby had always been there and he'd only now begun to explore it. Beauford didn't know.

"I ain't no got-damnt psycholanist." he was fond of saying. He said it even then as he thought of the bitch he had tied up in his basement. He'd fuck her good as soon as he walked through the door. He wouldn't even take a shower. He knew his smell revolted her. He felt her heaving when he pressed his naked flesh against her. She vomited once and to be honest, it just made it better. Her revulsion, her horror, it fed him. It made him harder, if that was even possible. That night went extra long.

Beauford ran his hands over his large round gut and reached down to adjust himself. It'd be hell driving the truck if his rod didn't go back to its flaccid bean-like rest position. He walked out of the large warehouse and made his way towards his truck. He raised a hand to his boss, Hector Rivera, and smiled even as he cursed having to work for a "fuck-hole wetback."

"Any plans tonight, Beauford?" Hector smiled at him as he pulled an envelope from his briefcase.

"No sir. Just a quiet evening at home." Beauford smiled back and accepted the check Hector handed him.

"That sounds like a plan, Stan." Hector patted Beauford on the shoulder.

"It's Beauford, Mr. Rivera."

"What?"

"You called me Stan. My name is Beauford."

"Oh no, Beauford. That's just a saying. You've worked for me over two years. You think I'd forget your name?"

"I'd like to rip your dick off and shove it up your ass you brown piece of shit."

"Beauford?"

Beauford blinked and smiled. His imagination had again gotten the best of him.

"Sorry, Mr. Rivera, guess my mind was already home on the couch with a cold beer."

"Mine is headed that way, son." Hector smiled again. It made him look much younger than he was.

Beauford returned the smile and added a wave before hauling himself into his truck.

Penetration. Yes. Beauford smiled. This wasn't the smile reserved for his boss. This was Beauford's real smile. The one the exposed the true madness that rested under the surface. This is the smile that reflected his hunger and right now, Beauford was starving.

**

Penetration.

That was the thought that got Mary-Anne Macarthy through her days. It didn't start that way. At first, it was god that helped her survive this nightmare. It was his name that she called out at night and whispered softly under her breath when Beauford was sliding over her and thrusting himself into her. Once the third week ticked away and Beauford started with his knives, god slipped from her mind.

For a while she just wanted to die. Her body was ruined, especially after the knife play began. She was no good to him anymore. How could she be? Her flesh was a map of slices, some spelling out his name like she was his property. Her breasts were badly infected, probably from the spittle he slathered them with after he cut them. She was a shell, her former beauty gone and the confidence that she was so well known for was destroyed. No amount of money that she or her family had would bring it back. She felt guilty for dwelling on her looks and maybe that's why she was in this position. Was she being punished for being prideful? Certainly, the good things she did with her money would balance out her proudness. She couldn't think of that now. Now her mind had to belong to that word.

Her mantra.

Penetration.

She would do to him what he enjoyed doing to her so often. Penetrate him. Deeply.

Across the cold stone basement, gleaming like a star, even in the dim light, was one of Beauford's toys. It had fallen off the table after one of his sessions and by some miracle, enough of a miracle in fact to let god slip back into her mind, he hadn't noticed it. It was a knife. Long, serrated but best of all sharp. She knew it was sharp because she had felt it drag across her body, tearing her flesh like soft bread.

But her prize was so far. Mary-Anne was tied with her arms above her head to a rusty pipe. The rope clung to her wrists biting with the slightest of movements. She was without hope, and even the promise of plunging that beautiful blade into the filthy fat flesh that hung off Beauford's bent skeleton wasn't enough to loosen the ropes that bound her.

"Mommy?"

Mary-Anne's eyes snapped open at the sound of the little girl. She scanned the room but she was alone.

"Mommy, please come home. Please I'm sorry I broke the cup."

At once, Mary-Anne was transported out of that dark basement and into the plush comfort of her home. She saw herself standing in the kitchen holding a shattered coffee mug. It was old, significant in that it was her long dead, but still grieved, mother's favorite mug.

The little girl was her daughter Maggie. She had tears in her blue eyes. Her black hair was pulled into a pony tail. Mary-Anne noticed a strand had come loose. She wondered if it resembled her mind by now.

"You have no idea how important this was to me you little brat. Go to your room! I can't stand to look at you!"

Back in the basement, Mary-Anne winced at the memory. It stung worse than the wounds that covered her body.

Maggie had run off then leaving Mary-Anne alone with the shattered cup and her simmering rage. She heard the sobs break free seconds before the slamming of a door.

Beauford had snatched Mary-Anne just hours later.

"Oh Maggie," Mary-Anne whispered, "I'm sorry."

She began pulling at the ropes. They were so tight each movement was like fire against her already raw skin but she had to continue. It was now or never. She might not get this drive back. She needed to be free, and to do that, she would have to bleed.

Beauford sat at the drive-through window of Cluckie's, his favorite chicken restaurant. He was staring intently at the missing poster that featured his plaything. He absently licked his lips, but whether that was from memory or from the smell of chicken wafting out of the window, he couldn't be sure. He barely noticed when Jimmy Jack Bryer came to the window to collect Beauford's hard earned cash. In fact, he had called his name three times before Beauford realized he was even there.

"Yo' Beauford! Wake up man we got a line."

"What? Oh." Beauford thrust the money into Jack's hand.

"What's wrong man? You losing it?"

"Fuck you say to me?" Beauford turned beat red, "Just what the fuck did you say?

"Yo relax dude!"

"You faggot! I'll fucking rip your heart out!" Beauford was struggling to lean out the window of his truck but his girth was holding him back, "I'll strangle you, you piece of shit!"

Jack shoved the bag of food into his hand.

"Enjoy your diabetes, you fat fuck." He slammed the window shut. He kept Beauford's change.

Were it possible, Beauford turned an even darker shade of red, but his voice had left him. He simply stared through the window, his eyes locked with Jack's. After a moment he took a breath and slid back into his car. He started to pull away.

Jack sent him off with a middle finger.

Beauford was fuming. That little piss-ant talking to him like that? Asking if he was losing it? Beauford slammed his hand against the steering wheel.

The radio was chattering about some type of industrial accident in Montana instead of pumping out his classic rock, so Beauford snapped it off. He didn't give a shit about what was happening across the country. He slammed his hand again.

Penetration.

Yes. That word again.

Beauford began to calm. He had his chicken and he had a bitch waiting for him. He had everything he needed.

He sped up.

***

Mary-Anne could not hold back her cry as her hand slipped free of the rope. It was one both of pain, as a substantial part of the flesh on her wrist had been sacrificed to the endeavor, and triumph as she was finally free. She frantically began untying her other hand. She couldn't get her fingers to grip the rope. There was too much blood. She tried to wipe it away on the cool cement.

"I'm coming, baby. I'm coming." Finally, she was able to grip the rope and slip the knot loose. When the rope fell to the ground and her arms were finally able to drop into her lap she almost wept. This couldn't be true. She was free of the ropes and one step closer to being free of *him*.

A low rumble filled the air. The garage door.

She knew this meant Beauford was home. He would come inside and eat his chicken first. Then he would start on her. She just didn't know how much time that meant. Often, he would eat down here in front of her, forcing her to watch him gnaw his way through a carton of chicken. The thought of him sucking the juices off his fat fingers was enough to send her dizzy with nausea. She shook her head free of the thought. It didn't matter when he came down. She only needed to stand up and get that knife. She struggled to her feet and was rewarded with agonizing pain as the cuts on her soles split open. Mary-Anne clamped her hands over her mouth to keep from crying out in pain. Instead, twin tears rolled down her cheeks.

Slowly, tentatively, she took a step. The white hot pain that ripped through her body didn't have a place she could say was the start. It seemed to radiate from everywhere. Her feet, her breasts, her legs, even her hands all at once ignited with an excruciating wave of agony. The strength fled in a heartbeat and Mary-Anne felt herself falling. Her head cracked against the cement and all she knew was stars before the sweet, cold darkness swallowed her whole.

***

Beauford sat down at his filthy kitchen table. He knocked aside empty beer cans and disgusting plates of half rotted food to clear space for his dinner. He pulled out his food slowly, almost ritualistically, first pausing to inhale the savory scent of the deep fried chicken. He tossed the plastic bag aside and ripped the lid off the carton. He immediately snatched a leg from the carton and tore into it like a starved animal. He had fun to have tonight and he wanted to be energized as quickly and completely as possible. In seconds, his fingers were slick with grease and specks of meat, but he ate on. First a leg, then a wing, a thigh, a breast (he took his time with that one) and another leg. Finally, the carton was empty and the chicken was devoured. Beauford relaxed in his chair with a heavy sigh. He wanted a nap, just a quick catnap before his fun began. His eyelids grew heavy and Beauford was on the edge of that sweet precipice where sleep waited to catch you when you dropped.

But no. He slammed his hand on the table, "Wake up, you old hound dog!" he shouted. He had fun to have, while it lasted. He'd made the decision on his way home. This would be the last weekend for his houseguest. This time he wouldn't hold back.

The basement door opened with a long and deep groan. He liked it that way. It was his own little alarm system right here on the basement door. He stepped into the landing and pulled the door shut behind him. Fifteen steps down to his bliss and he was down them quickly. Despite having just wolfed down nearly an entire chicken, his mouth was watering heavily. He was hungry, that deep kind of hungry that food never touched. He licked his lips as he stepped off the bottom step and into the basement.

It took him a moment to realize what he was seeing. His brain was struggling to comprehend what his eyes were showing him.

He shuffled forward, a low whine rising from his gut. His toy was gone. All that remained was the bloodied rope.

But Mary-Anne was not gone. Not then, not yet. She was slowly rising behind Beauford. She was sitting beneath the table when he clamored down the stairs. He didn't even notice her there. He didn't notice her holding the large blade either. Not until she slipped it through the layers of fat that hung off his back.

As the blade slipped easily into him, Beauford's eyes widened. The pain started like a pinprick but as the sharp (and it was sharp Beauford, always made sure his knives were sharp), knife tore its way through his back the pain spread and engulfed him.

His howl of agony was sweet medicine to Mary-Anne's ears. She pushed the knife further in and Beauford fell to his knees. She pushed him forward and he collapsed onto his hands. She yanked out the knife and jammed it in again.

Penetration.

There was a sadistic smile on Mary-Anne's face as she pulled the knife out again. Her eyes surveyed the wounds, the flowing blood, and rested on Beauford's rotund ass. She moved almost like a reflex without thought or consideration. Her arm swung back and she struck. Quickly, deeply. The blade cut through the soft flesh easily, ripping into him, penetrating him, destroying.

His scream was animalistic.

She left the knife in him and stepped towards his head. She leaned forward and whispered softly, "Who's fucked now?" She ripped the knife out of him. A river of shit and blood flowed after it, oozing from the wreckage she left behind. She raised the knife again. It was filthy with Beauford's waste and gore. It was then that everything she had been subjected to, the pain, the rapes, the agony, was unleashed. With a howl she struck. Over and over she stabbed him. She ripped away at him, penetrating his fat flesh over and over. Even as her voice grew horse and her arms tired she penetrated him.

Finally, the pain in her arms forced her to stop. She slammed the knife into him one final time. She stood there covered in the gore of her captor watching him. She wanted to be sure he was really dead. Despite the river of blood that covered the floor, deep enough to hide her feet. Despite the chunks of flesh and bone scattered around her, she had to be sure.

She stood there for hours and Beauford never moved. Finally, she turned away.

Penetration.

She had done it. Over and over she had pierced him, ripped him open, unleashing the horror she had experienced these past weeks. Now it was finished.

Now she was free.

It was well past dark when she emerged from Beauford's house. Despite her disgust, she had rummaged through his closet to find a shirt that did not stink of him, so she was not traveling a bloody naked mess. She didn't need to worry however; the streets were quiet and empty.

She sobbed slightly as she stepped out into the cool air. She wiped the tears from her bloodied cheeks and walked on. The trip did not take long. Beauford lived only a couple miles from her own house. To know she was so close only added to the agony. Each step sent stabs of pain up her legs as the asphalt bit into her shredded feet. It was no matter. Each step just confirmed she was alive and pushed her towards home.

Finally, she turned down her street. It looked so peaceful, even shrouded in darkness. She began to run. Bloody footprints marked her path as she ran.

"Maggie!" She screamed, her voice hoarse. There it was, just ahead. Her home. Her sanctuary. She darted up the walk, not noticing the yellow tape streaming in the gentle wind. She threw herself at the door. She pounded on it, "Please. Please open up. Maggie? Derek? Please."

She reached above her head and quickly unscrewed the porch light cover. Taped to the ceiling was a key. She jumped and yanked it loose. She pushed the key into the lock and opened the door.

What struck her first was the smell. It was not the fresh lavender scent she used to spray around the house. This was thick, coppery. She knew it immediately.

"No…no…"

Her husband Derek was killed in the kitchen. The tape outline of his sprawled body still remained. The floor, even in the dark, still held the brownish stain of his blood. Mary-Anne spun around and vomited. It was all dry heaving and spit but the pain in her stomach was excruciating. With a feral like moan she rushed out of the kitchen and up the stairs to the second floor.

"Maggie? Baby?" She knew what she would find, but still she was unprepared. The tape outline of her daughter was at the center of her bedroom. Toys were scattered around the room. Her small twin bed was untouched. The blood blossomed around the tape like angel's wings.

Mary-Anne fell to her knees and curled up beside the shape of her daughter.

She wept quietly and gently caressed the empty floor .

Beauford must have come back sometime after he had taken her. He had returned and taken her family from her. Penetrating her one last time, even in death.

That was that for Mary-Anne. She cried softly as the strength drained from her body. What did she have to live for? What was left?

She would slip away and join them soon. It wouldn't be long now...

Not long at all.

In the dim light of dawn, the basement of Beauford's house seemed to glow a dull grey. The air scattered with dust particles that floated undisturbed. So it was before the large black book materialized and fell to the ground with a resounding thud. Immediately, black smoke swirled into the room and formed the shape of a man. A scythe sparked against the cement as Malachai, Lord of the Reapers and newly ascended Lucifer, stepped forward.

"Beauford Bixby. Such a monster to walk the earth."

He waved his hand and chunks of flesh scattered around the room began to shiver and move across the floor.

"You walk the earth no longer. You are in my realm now. I have much use for you."

The book opened and the pages began turning rapidly.

"Your name shall be written amongst my army. The Book of Names holds your loyalty."

Beauford's eyes snapped open.

"Beauford Bixby. Rise as one of my Choir."

Thick black wings burst from Beauford's back. His fingers split open and thick shards of gleaming metal slide forward. His teeth are jagged and sharp.

"Your cruelty is exquisite." Malachai grinned, "I shall unleash it."

The Book of Names slammed shut.